THE STATE WITNESS

THE STATE WITNESS

SHAUKAT OSMAN

Translated from the Bangla by Osman Jamal

PEEPAL TREE

First published in Great Britain in 1993
Peepal Tree Books
17 King's Avenue
Leeds LS6 1QS
England

© Shaukat Osman 1986, 1993
Translation © Osman Jamal 1993

All rights reserved
No part of this publication may be
reproduced or transmitted in any form
without permission

ISBN 0 948833 58 0

Peepal Tree gratefully acknowledges Arts Council support

The State Witness
is dedicated to the memory of
Sanjib Dutta (from Bangladesh)
and A.L. Khatib (from Maharashtra)

CHAPTER ONE

Of course my parents gave me a name. Saburan, meaning patience. They must have known I'd have to wait, be patient, even if there is nothing to look forward to. My mother saw to it that I learnt patience from the age of two. She just took herself from the world so she wouldn't be there when I called. Someone else did though. *Bap* brought home a mother. Mine, not his. I was lucky. I was spared the usual stepmotherly treatment. My second mother was a good person. She may not have loved me from the heart, but she never treated me badly. Good luck I'd call it for I could have had hell from the age of two. That came when I was eleven. When I look back, memories blur but they haven't gone completely. As I sit alone in this prison cell, I often wonder why people have to suffer so much. And it's other people who cause it. As a peasant girl what did I want? A fistful of rice when I was hungry, two pieces of cloth, and something to put my head under so that in the rain, the cold and the wind, people wouldn't come snatching at my legs. Was it too much to ask? It's a strange world. People want different things, and who can say who needs what? People mix up needs and wants. They have enough to eat, but they aren't satisfied with a fistful of rice, they want more. I don't know why. Perhaps I would if I were in their shoes. But, by Allah, when I *did* have my fistful of rice, I could never hang on to it for long. If I could, there'd be no need to tell you my story and I tell you, I've been ground down so much I feel I've become an old woman over the last ten or twelve years. But how old am I? Bap used to say I was ten or eleven when the Muktijuddho war started. I remember those days. I don't suppose I can be much over twenty-five now. Yet I feel ready for the grave. I tell you, I've had it up to here with life. I keep looking at the walls of this cell. The eyes of the bricks are as hard as any which have looked at me since my childhood. I don't think there's any feeling left in my heart either. Otherwise how could I ever forget my bap. I don't know if he's dead or alive. Yet all I'd wanted was that I'd be happy, make Bap happy, have a man of my own and enough to eat from my own bit of land. Nothing more. That's the truth or I'm a streetwalker's daughter. No, I didn't ask for any more at Allah's court. What do I want now? I don't know any more. It's one thing to be inside the jail, another outside. Only Allah knows when I'll get out of this place. The police said, 'You tell the truth and you've got nothing to fear. You'll be free to go.' They have others to punish. They've got nothing against a woman like me. They're after those who put us on this road. But how this case turns out depends on my testimony. If I tell lies, the accused will get off the hook. If that happens the police will be annoyed with me. That's what they told me. I gave straightforward answers to their questions; I didn't play around with the truth. There's nothing untrue in what I said. That's why they're so kind to me. They said I didn't have to stay in custody, they'd provide me with an escort to wherever I wanted to go. But who have I got in this city — except the accused himself? Where would I go? The police said it would be all right as long as I appeared in court on the dates of hearing. But if I failed to appear, they'd have to fetch me. To which hell out there would I go? Allah knows in whose trap I'd fall again if I did. I've passed through so many hands during the last six years before I landed here, I thought I'd better stay put. Of course it's not much fun in here, but at least I'm safe. I wasn't born rich. I'd started running errands for my stepmother when I was two and a half and carried my father's dinner to the field from the age of four. People used to say I'd grow to be a brave girl. Well, I haven't. I went out to take on my fate, I didn't want to get thrashed by it, and I thought one day Allah would look kindly on me. I won't blame Him. He did look kindly on me. I thought if I could spend a year or two like this, I'd save some money, get some jewellery. Then I'd leave this place, get one of my own and Bap would come to live with me. He'd choose the right man for me and I wouldn't have wanted any say in the matter. I'd buy a bit of land with my savings. But that wasn't to be. I'll say this, though, I ate well in the job. You don't find food like that in the country and it's fun eating in the curtained cubicles of a restaurant. But then that's part of the job and, as they say, every job's different. You need a plough and bulls and such like to work the fields but they're not much good in the kitchen. There you need choppers and pots. Well, you know what I'm saying. The things you 'need' vary with the work you're doing. That's something I learned when I came to work in town. You don't learn everything right away. Some learn slowly, others fast. I stayed in a bustee when I first came to town and I learned a lot in two years. At first I couldn't send any money to Bap, but I soon made contacts. I sent him quite a bit of money, more than he expected. Then I lost touch with him again, though he still used to get the money. Whatever else my patron was, he wouldn't swindle me out of a mere fifty taka. I was pleased that whatever I might have done or become, I'd come closer to Bap. Nothing else would have made me happier. Putting a smile on a sad face, well, it raises your spirits, makes you feel good. I had that comfort, but still I wonder if there wasn't another way to earn a living. I saved some money in the last two years. I saved it with this man who used to say, 'Saburan, I'm putting your money in the bank for you. And if I ever swindle the poor, let that day be my last day.' Allah knows you could trust him. To look at, you wouldn't think he was an evil man. He had a handsome round face, a black beard but no moustache. You wouldn't think he was anything but pious. But he had his odd ways. He had dealings with women, usually young ones. Only one or two were as old as their thirties — but he didn't seem to have an appetite for any of them. I can say with my hand on the Quran, as I sit in this cell, that the man's heart matched his looks. It's not for nothing that I trusted him. I often tried my charm on him, resting my silken eyes on his face. Let him hold out his hands, I thought, and take me in his arms. But he remained stone cold. Most girls who joined us stayed for only ten, fifteen or so days. I stuck it out for three years for him. I felt that he didn't see young women as more than things, kitchen tools like pestles, pots or pans. He didn't mind when I went out with a man. He would say, 'Well, you need the money, and so do I.' I still don't know how I stuck it out there so long. Others came and went but my guardian couldn't find me another job. Others left as soon as jobs were found for them, but when I asked for one, he'd say, 'Saburan, the point is to earn a living. Does it matter where you do it?' I didn't know then where those who did go went and what they were up to. Now I know everything and I'll come to that later. Bap got me married the year after the Mutkijuddho war. He was a young man, my husband, but I was only eleven or twelve, and I didn't appreciate the value of a man. When in time I did, I thought just such a man and a piece of land would be enough to make the world beautiful. But one day he left and never returned. Bap went looking for him. His parents cried their eyes out. I'd become fond of him, yet he deceived me, but then my acquaintance with misery was nothing new. My stepmother often went to work for the Miahs. Bap had no land of his own, so he worked for others. I often took his dinner to the fields. Bap made this arrangement to have the whole of his daily wage in cash. Otherwise food was supplied by those for whom one worked, but then that meant a reduced wage which Bap didn't like. When I first went to the Miahs I was amazed. I didn't know then that people lived like that and they needed so many things and of such great variety. The women folk of the Miahs didn't go out and yet they wore such pretty clothes. I used to tell my stepmother that I'd buy pretty clothes when I grew up. She used to laugh. Now I know why she laughed. But I'll tell you this, the clothes I wear now are better than those the women of the Miahs wore. I've changed a lot. I'm surprised when I look at myself. When I was in my village home, I barely glanced at myself in a broken mirror. Now that I've learnt the language of the sahibs, I admire myself in front of a dressing table. Bap's income couldn't support us. In the rainy season, after the harvest, he was often out of work. My stepmother was a sensible woman; she joined in the struggle for survival. I accompanied her to the Miahs. Who could I stay at home with? There was a small pond near our house and Bap was afraid that I might drown in it. I often played with the other young children round there. Bap went out even if he didn't have a job to go to. It helped even if he only picked up a branch or two for firewood. If you're poor, an empty belly's the same whatever village you come from. Bap sometimes went fishing in the river with a bamboo net. If he caught a big fish, he sold it in the market and bought rice, lentils, salt and chillies. Sometimes he was too ill to go to work. If my stepmother didn't have a job at the Miahs, only Allah knows what would have happened. I don't like to remember those days. But the walls of this prison can't keep those memories out, and they come rushing in whether I want them to or not. The past won't leave me in peace. There was this middle-aged woman, whom we called Khala because she was like a mother's sister, who joined us here. Her case hadn't yet come up for hearing. Khala lived in the city; she had done for the last twenty years. She was tough. And funny. She was caught stealing but she wouldn't admit it. 'Khala', I said. 'Yes, niece,' she replied and laughed for no reason. 'Go on,' she said, 'What is it?' 'You were caught thieving, why did you tell them you hadn't done it ?' 'Oh, you're young, you won't understand. Everybody's at it — thieving, though you can't call it mere thieving if you're caught. If you are it's seen as robbery.' Khala was a funny woman. She'd been jailed many times for thieving, but there wasn't a trace of guilt in her. She brushed away the difficulties of prison life as if they were fairy tales. She had a firm figure like mine. She must have been over forty, but she was still strong. And, by Allah, she had a tongue as sharp as a knife. I've never been to court before, so I tremble when I think what I should say in reply to the magistrate's questions. But Khala gave me courage. She said, 'It's all right if you take your time to think up an answer. You can pretend to be deaf, holding your hand over your ear like the hood of a cobra.' Sitting around with Khala was fun. When you felt miserable, she'd brush it all away. One day I said, 'You've had it, haven't you, if you're caught thieving. The question is, how many months you're going to get for it.' Khala laughed her head off. As she wouldn't stop laughing, I made to get up and go. 'I won't speak to you again,' I said. She grabbed me by the hand and had another laugh. 'Can't I have a laugh, Saburan? Well, there's nothing to worry over. They'll clap me in jail for six months or a year. That's all. I don't care about that.' 'But why?' 'You're young, you won't understand. I'll go to jail, that's all there is to it. They'll give me food. The jailer will make me work, let him. At least he'll give me food to eat. I'll work and get food for my work. What's there to be scared of? When I'm out and working, I often go hungry. And there are times when I don't even have a job. Well then? It's better this way.' When she burst into laughter after that, how could I be annoyed with her? I can't remember my mother, but I'd found a mother in her. Prisoners wait in custody and some don't get a hearing date for months on end. I hardly ever talk to them. But it was a pleasure to hang around Khala. You could hear such odd things. Once she said, 'You know, dear, they don't all come here for thieving. Some may've killed, some may've had a fight and there are others who may've done nothing at all.' 'How's that?' I said, surprised. 'Yes, even good people can get sent to jail. I'll tell you what happened a few years ago. That time, too, I was caught nicking. I shoplifted where I used to buy my mistress's toilet things. I touched the shopkeeper's hands and feet, asking his forgiveness. Of course I didn't *quite* touch his feet and how could I put my hand in his? I mean, he wasn't my man, was he?' Khala let go her unstoppable laughter before going on. 'Just a figure of speech, dear. But the man was a butcher, there was no kindness in his heart. He handed me over to the police. I told the magistrate I was guilty, but he too was a butcher, and he plied his knife. Six months!' I interrupted: 'You were telling me how good people who haven't done anything wrong are jailed too.' 'Thanks for reminding me,' Khala said. 'One of the prisoners was a girl who could read and write. Dark, but pretty. I called her sister. The other girl was a Hindu and I called her Didi, the Hindu word for sister. They both came from good families and when they spoke, their words were honey sweet. I was in for six months. They call us extras. You know they make you work in jail. My job was to run errands for those girls. Well, what was I to do for them? It was they who ran errands for me. One day they said, Auntie — they called me Auntie — Auntie, your hair needs oiling, it looks dry. I could have disappeared into the ground in shame. These girls from good families, could I let them oil my hair? Oh, help me, God! But they wouldn't listen to my protest. They oiled my hair and combed it. They washed their own clothes, they wouldn't let me do it. They said, 'You know, Auntie, people who do wrong aren't wholly to blame; responsibility also lies with the country and society in which the wrongdoer lives.' I couldn't understand much of what they said, but I couldn't admit I didn't, could I? I wasn't clever enough, I just nodded my head and said yes yes. They thought I understood. They were very good, those girls. I really had no work to do, apart from talking to those girls. One of them said, 'It's your own country that makes a thief of you and then cries thief. Not everybody steals. Well, then, why not?' They told me, 'Auntie, you don't have to work for us. We, too, are women, we can do all the usual chores. You'd better learn to read and write.' An old old crone like me learn to read and write? I couldn't stop laughing, but they wouldn't listen. So I started with the name of the *pir*. Wait a minute. Let me have a laugh.' Then followed waves of laughter. 'Khala, stop,' I said. 'Did you learn to read and write?' She gently slapped herself on both cheeks. 'I got going. The girls got me a slate and pencils. Whose children were they? They had such golden tongues and so much kindness for a woman like me!' Khala stopped and said after a moment's thought, 'They told me odd things. They said people didn't know themselves; they wouldn't go bad if they did. Because they didn't know who they were, they became thieves, murderers, robbers, conmen. The poor didn't know why they were poor, so they remained poor and suffered. I didn't understand a lot of what they said; I only remember one or two things. But I loved listening to them, those darling girls.' Khala's face went dark as she spoke. Her laughter stopped, her face fell and I could see the lines of age on it. As she sighed, she said, 'Saburan, darling, it's a strange world and people are even more so. I was very fond of those girls. I soon learned the alphabet and they said I was very clever. 'You're learning so quickly', they said, 'you won't take long, you'll soon learn to read and write.' But my luck had run out. The girls were taken to another jail. I cried the day they left. Even now when I remember them, I feel empty inside my heart.' I often wondered how Khala had started stealing. She'd become a mother to me. There are always little problems in prison. She did all she could, like a mother. 'If you were my daughter, would I have sat back?' she said. I once asked her, 'You say you can't help thieving. Did you nick from those girls you talk about, who taught you to read and write?' 'God forbid,' she said, 'How could I nick from them? They were sinless like angels. But I did put away two of their hairclips, of plastic or whatever, very cheap. I stick them in my hair when ever I get back to prison but put them away in a little case when I'm out. I'd have become a real person if I'd stayed with them. I left my book, my slate and pencils in prison when I got out. What should I do with them? Who'd ever teach me again with such sympathy and care?' There were many in prison who loved Khala. However unhappy we were, she'd think of something funny and then we'd all laugh. She had no equal in making fun of the guard. When the doctor came to see a patient, she would say, 'Don't give us any medicine, doctor. Give us a little poison.' 'Poison is medicine,' the doctor said, to which Khala replied, 'Doctor, you've learnt so much for nothing. There's a medicine called poison. Why do you beat about the bush when you've only got that one to give.' Khala had guts; she could bandy words with the senior jail doctor. Later she said, 'Saburan, people take poison when they can't find food. There isn't much poison in the world, but that's what they run after. One should think of food. I come to jail for it.' Then Khala was given a date for her hearing. When she was about to leave she said, 'Don't worry. I'll be back. Food is scarce out there.' I was heartbroken. For a few days the prison felt like hell, even though our guardians in the city had us kept in comfort. We lived two or three to a room, with attached baths. I tell you when I came to prison, I didn't suffer much inconvenience. I thought about my father and my bed in our village home. We had two small bamboo-walled rooms, where we also kept our pots and pans and various household articles. Each room had only one small window, so we got stewed in the heat. Had the slave girl changed into a princess? Well, I hadn't lost my head. I knew what it was like to live in a bustee — and one in the city at that. There are bustees in the country, many small huts huddled together with alleys running between them. But, oh Allah, what did I see when I first came to the city? It was Chacha, a village uncle, who'd said to my father: 'There isn't much you can do about a poor man's lot. Yet one should move on. The girl is unfortunate, she's lost her man. Allah knows if he's alive. Well, do something, send her to town. At least there'll be one fewer mouth to feed. You may even receive some money every month.' Chacha told Bap about a similar case in the next village. Bap agreed. I'd already made up my mind. True, there'd be one fewer mouth to feed. Bap and my stepmother lived half-starved. Poor Ma! She had no children of her own, but she gave me no trouble and I was fond of her. I agreed to go. I hoped to send Bap some money after a month or two. I'd probably get ten to fifteen taka as my wages and I'd heard that sahibs gave away clothes as gifts. I could send them to my stepmother. She'd be glad to have them. I was annoyed with myself. If I were a boy I'd have been useful to my parents long ago. 'When are you going?' Bap asked. 'The day after tomorrow.' 'You want to take her with you, but she'll need money for fares.' 'Don't worry about that. I'll pay now; she can pay me back when she receives her wages.' I looked at Bap's face and knew how anxious he was. As it all keeps coming back, I feel empty inside my chest. Ma cried when I set off; her tears wouldn't stop. Do people feel so strongly for a stepdaughter? And me? I felt darkness all around me, made even deeper by my tears. Bap burst out crying when I touched his feet. Six or seven years have passed since I last saw him. My heart feels restless. I'd hoped to go back to bap for the rest of my life. I didn't want to stay in town any longer. I believe Bap still receives money every month, but I don't hear from him. Qazi sahib is a trustworthy man. My suspicion is unwarranted, my mind disturbed. Getting back to the bustee — Allah, it was sheer hell. A bustee in the country is nothing like it. There, at least, one doesn't worry about the toilet. One can always go behind a bush. Travelling to town, railway trains, rickshaws, they were all new to me. I hadn't seen them before. I looked about in fear, and when I saw Chacha's house I nearly collapsed. We'd arrived at night and I was feeling a bit dizzy, so I didn't see more than what was visible in the evening light. But what sort of a house was this? A cowshed in the country was better. I had a good look at the place the next morning. There were rows of huts along the railway line. You had to crawl to get into them. Some were made of plaited bamboo, but others were made out of anything people could lay their hands on. Apart from the water in the ditch by the railway line, there was a water tap down the road, but you had to walk some distance to get to it for drinking water. Chacha had come to town long ago, living with Chachi and their two children. Why, but for a fistful of rice, had he left his village? You can't cling to your hearth and home if you are starving for months on end. They had just one room — if you'd call it a room — but it was biggish. We all slept in there. I slept in a corner next to the two children, eight and ten years old. I could scarcely sleep. I felt as if I was lying in my grave and the torments of hell had started. I felt like crying when I went to the latrine. They'd built something like a high platform over the roadside ditch with jute sacking hung round it for walls. It was open to the sky. Who knows if the passengers of the trains running on the high ground didn't cast their eyes through the the opening. You had to be very careful going up to the seat. Water plants grew in the ditch water you had to wade through to climb on to the platform. I was so distressed I didn't want to stay there for another day. I wanted to go home. I felt it better to starve there than live in that hell. Chachi's words lightened my heart a little. She said, 'Do you think we're happy here? But then it's town and you don't go without a job for long. Allah provides so you get a little something to eat. Do you think we left our home just like that? First your Chacha came, then he brought us along. When I first came here I just cried and cried. Now I've got used to it.' They'd suffered but their lot hadn't got better. I swore to myself that I wouldn't let it happen to me. Well, I had guts then. A week passed. Chacha had a job as a builder's labourer. I hadn't seen a city before. There were rows of buildings and hundreds more were being built. Chacha said there was no shortage of jobs at the moment. But I was an extra mouth to feed, so he had to find me a job. I'd seen a lot in seven days. Their ten-year-old child went to school in the bustee. He showed me around at the weekend. Everything looked strange to me, yet things weren't really that different. Here, too, people fought with their destiny. Nobody had anything to spare. Given the chance people stole. As they had nothing, people quarrelled about little things. All night men and women shouted and screamed. One day two mothers tangled over their children's tiffs and the fathers joined in. But there were elders and good neighbours who came forward and brought peace. As kerosene was dear, we went to bed early. Chacha had his meal when he returned from work and we joined him. Then after a brief rest in the small yard, we went to bed. But I could hardly sleep. When my eyes were shut, my mind ran about. What was in store for me? I had no answer to that, but I thanked Allah for keeping me well. I didn't want to be even more of a burden. I got to know one or two girls in the area. They asked me where I'd come from, if my parents were alive, why I'd come to town, if I was married and why had my husband run away? I didn't like answering such questions. One day a woman came to visit Chachi. She was more like a man really. She had a massive neck and a booming voice. Chachi offered her paan. When she saw me, she asked her who I was. 'My niece,' Chachi said. The big, fat woman left after a while. I couldn't sleep that night although it was quiet. Late at night I heard whispering voices. I pricked up my ears. Chachi was speaking. There was only the one room. She thought I was asleep. 'Try and get rid of the girl soon,' she said. 'Why,' Chacha said. 'That fat woman came today. She's made trouble for the whole bustee. You've taken the responsibility for someone else's daughter. Well, find a job for her. Can you quarrel with that woman with all those *goondas* behind her? The girl's young, she's fresh, lively, she's got good looks. I swear by Allah that woman has her eyes on our niece. You've taken the responsibility, you've got to see that she gets back home with her honour.' Chacha didn't answer at once. 'You're right,' he said. 'The poor get no peace, do they? When people come to town starving, you should try and help them. But what happens? If they come with the torment of the stomach, the bastards here receive them with the torment of their pricks.' I remembered my runaway husband. He loved me, but then what happened to him? Why did he abandon me like this? It was he who got me into this. I was angry. If he was gone, good riddance! I didn't want to see him again. I thought if only I could save some money, I'd pass the rest of my life with Bap. I'd have liked to go back to my village. Oh, Allah, get me back to my village home! I realised from what Chacha said that another kind of business thrived here. I'd thought that Chacha and Chachi were older people, they would protect me, what did I have to fear? But Chachi's words deflated me. The fat woman had goondas working for her. What did they do? Did they carry people away by force? It wouldn't take long to cut through the bamboo wall. But there were lights on in town. Not like the country where it got dark after evening and thieves, robbers and other bad elements took advantage. Could that sort of thing happen in town? I couldn't go to sleep again. I thought I'd talk to Chachi in the morning. Then I felt shy. How could you talk about these things with your elders? God forbid! That fat woman came again after two or three days, but a job was found for me— may Allah have mercy on Chacha— in a gentleman's house in the west side of the town. The sahib had recently moved house and he needed someone to work in his new household. Chacha, may Allah be kind to him, was a pious man. He taught me much. If you live in town you have to remember addresses. The number and name of the street and the area. It's hard to find a house if you don't know its number. 'It's not like in the country where everybody knows everybody else,' he said. 'It's a city. Many people, many houses, much wealth and also many sins. Keep your head, dear. People come to town looking for food. Otherwise, would anybody leave their ancestral home?' I sometimes feel sorry for Chacha. We live in the same town, yet we haven't seen each other for ages. I don't know if they're still there. I've drunk from many ghats and met many people, but I don't want to think about all that now. I've got into such a mess I can't even write to Bap. I still can't read and write. I could get someone to write for me. You can get people to do anything for you if you've got money. In any case, whatever my patron Qazi may do, he won't deceive me. He too wanted to earn a little money and have a quiet life. He really did look after me for the last four years and I did whatever he told me to do. You can never tell when life, like river Padma, is going to overflow. I think my kindly feelings are drying up inside me. I'd all but forgotten my father I'd become so self-centred. He chose the right name for me. Saburan, meaning patience. I can wait. But how long? Will I ever get out of here? The police said I wouldn't be punished if I told the truth in the court. Well, why should I be punished? I was only the butt of the knife. It's the one who uses the knife who's guilty. One of the prisoners here says she'd get off the hook if she had the right sort of witness. But I'll have to bear witness against my patron, Qazi. I hadn't really thought about that before. If I tell the truth, Qazi'll be jailed. What'll happen to me then? He keeps account for me. All I've got are two gold bangles, which were deposited at the prison gate. What if I don't get them back? Wouldn't it be an act of treachery if I got Qazi into trouble? I was lucky to find him. When Khala was here, I didn't think about him at all. I hear she's been jailed for a year on a theft charge. She's been sent to another jail. Will my boat sink now it's arrived? I can't understand what happened. Qazi used to say you mustn't panic in danger. The police have taken him into custody as well. If I could just see him once, I'd know what to do. They tell me I'll meet him in court in front of the magistrate. They won't let us talk. The defendant isn't allowed to answer questions put by lawyers or magistrates. Allah knows what'll happen. When I wake up in the middle of the night, my heart keeps twisting. I don't know what I can do. What would I have lost if I hadn't come to town? I'd have suffered want, wouldn't have had enough food to eat or clothes to wear. Would such sufferings have scalded my heart like this? If I tell the truth, it'd be an act of treachery. I don't know much about the man, who he really is and where he comes from, but I know I couldn't have dreamed of happiness without his kindness. What could I have done if I hadn't come to town? Once I got Bap to take me to my father-in-law's. He wouldn't agree at first. 'They're poor,' he said. 'Their son's run away. I doubt they'll support his wife.' I insisted: 'There's no harm in trying, Bap.' One day he had no job to go to, so he took me to my father-in-law's. Four miles wasn't far. I'd no proper veil, so I wrapped up in an old sari. It was the height of summer; I soon got soaked in sweat. Not far from the house of the in-laws, we sat down under a tree to rest. When our clothes were a little dry, we set off again. Allah knows what the state of my mind was. I'd been there twice before. Once on the day I got married; the other time I'd spent a fortnight there. Then two years had passed and they hadn't as much as looked me up. What could my bap do apart from blaming his fate? When we arrived at my father-in-law's, the first person I met was my mother-in-law. I was at the entrance to the inner yard when she saw me. It would have been natural for her to wonder who I was. I'd removed my veil, but three years had passed since she last saw me. Yet my mother-in-law hadn't forgotten me. Putting her arms round me, she cried loud and long. Women of the village came running at the noise she made. 'What a pretty wife and what charm! It's all fate or how could this happen?' I don't know who said it for I'd put my head down in embarrassment, but those words still ring in my ears. Bap found an excuse to leave immediately. My heart ached for him. He'd walked under the sun for an hour and a half and now he was in the sun again. Perhaps there was something in my father-in-law's manner. That became clear five days later. These people had a bit of land, which supported them for four months in a year. They had a two-room mud hut. Allah had found me a good home, but it was too good to last. My mother-in-law would have loved to keep me close to her bosom. I've never had so much affection showered on me. She used to fork out food from her own plate. 'Have one more fistful of rice, my dear,' she'd insist. It was enough to fill your heart as well as your stomach. But one night I heard my mother-in-law and my father-in-law arguing in a loud whisper in the next room. 'Will he ever come back? He's gone, setting fire to his hearth and home. Some son! Now what good is hanging on to her? Let her go back to her father.' 'You're an old man and she's your son's wife. She's ours now. If she loses her honour, it'll be our dishonour. Why don't you let her stay?' 'Don't forget it'll mean an extra mouth to feed. Then there's clothes, oil for her hair, her illnesses. I'm too old to take the burden.' 'Then *you* tell her. Drop her a hint. Say you'd like to see her father.' 'I can't.' 'Leave it then.' Bap came along before the week was over. Again he didn't touch anything in that house except a glass of water. No later than the time I took to get ready, we were back on the road. I can't forget my mother-in-law, who gave me an old sari and a blouse when I left, combed my hair for me and accompanied me to the entrance to the inner yard. When we got on to the road, I heard a loud cry, the same cry I'd heard when we came here.

Only this was louder and you could hear it from far away. All the way home, although the sound of the cry couldn't have reached that far, I heard nothing else. My eyes were blinded by tears. To spare Bap, I didn't sob, and then there were people on the road. But I couldn't walk properly. Bap was walking ahead of me and I kept falling further behind. When he hurried me, I tried to catch up, but it exhausted me. I couldn't eat for two days. Why had I gone to a place I falsely claimed to be my home? That home had turned into my grave. I felt as if I was no longer alive and walked the earth like a ghost. I learned to bear suffering. As I look back now, it must have been then that my heart turned into stone. How else could I have suffered the thousand misfortunes over the past years? Things are like a river in flood. Your fate depends on which side of the river you are on as you face the flood. If I'd met someone other than Qazi I'd have drowned or been swept along in a different way. What a man! He wouldn't be hooked; didn't seem to grasp the meaning of hints I gave him. I'd gone out with other people. I suppose elegance in dress is the easiest thing to achieve. It doesn't take long to learn if you've got money. In three years I changed into a lady. Nobody would have guessed I was only a country girl. I was not required to say much, for those who took me out didn't come to hear me talk. They came seized by a whim to take a woman to a hotel for the night. Qazi was helpful — the men went to him first. He knew all about it; I didn't do anything without his approval. Allah had put the man in my way when times were difficult. Chacha had found me a job and I'd moved from the bustee to a mansion. Built in spacious grounds, it had large rooms and such beautiful pink on the walls and such abundance of furniture, it soothed your eyes. And the kitchen was a magic world. So many types of crockery, of glass, china, silver. There was nothing of gold, but it all glittered like gold. It was hard to turn your eyes away. You didn't need firewood or kerosene for the cooker, it went on and off as you pressed a button. How convenient it all was! On the first day my eyes nearly popped out of my head. Then I got used to it all. I learned manners and many new expressions. Ashtray, dish, carpet, fridge and such like. Gradually I blended with the surroundings. By the kitchen there was a small room for the cook. Other servants slept elsewhere. I couldn't sleep the first night. They had no proper *baburchi*, only a female cook. I had to help her. My bed was beside hers and she snored. Some people in the city lived so comfortably. There were those in the country, like the women of the Miahs who were proud of their money and jewellry, but they would look like maid-servants here. May Allah be kind to Chacha, I'd at least live in comfort and, as the sahib told him, receive a wage of fifteen taka a month. This would help Bap. Besides, he wouldn't have to provide for me. Now I was of some use to my parents. Wasn't that something? So I said again and again, May Allah be good to Chacha! The mistress of the house was a good person, she was gentle. She told me off when I made mistakes, but didn't raise her voice. On the very first day I realised she was a kind-hearted person. 'You're from the country, aren't you?' she said. 'Perhaps you haven't got any clothes other than those you're wearing.' I stood there, looking down. I had a small bundle under my arm and a strip of cloth to wipe my hands and face. My mistress gave me two old saris and an old towel. 'Keep clean,' she said repeatedly. 'There's soap in the kitchen and there's a washroom next to it.' I still remember her. I've worked for five or six mistresses since. Some of them were female butchers, huffing and puffing in their own heat. One fat one couldn't get rid of her heat *in* the house, so she went out. And a sahib used to go out to get rid of *his* heat, so the memsahib took it out on her servants. The bitch seemed to be standing on a hot plate, leaping about day and night. Sometimes I felt like taking a hot poker to her whatsit. There were those who didn't consider servants human. So they had no names; they were someone's mother, gran or aunt. I still don't understand why these women of gentle birth who ate well, dressed well and had read a lot, failed to become human. They didn't work, but ate a lot, and I suppose as they were loath to move their bodies, bubbles formed in their bellies which then got to their genitals and tickled them and they went berserk. In town I discovered that people suffer from diseases of the mind and there are doctors to treat them. I'd never heard of it before. In one of these houses, the mistress, her daughter and even the master used to run to their mind doctor. They had no work to do, no sympathy for other people, they were only concerned about their bellies and genitals; no wonder they got sick. Now where have I got to? I can't keep my head. You can't think clearly when you're in pain. No, I haven't come across anyone else like my first mistress. I had to leave her after a year and a half. That's another story. But I can still see her in my mind's eye. Allah gave her a heart as great as her wealth. She looked after everybody. She asked me many questions. Were my parents alive? Why had my husband run away? What did my father, a landless labourer, do when he didn't have a job? She asked questions like kinfolk would. 'Sahib has fixed your wages at fifteen taka, I'll give you fifteen more,' she said. 'Send the lot to your father every month.' She surprised me. I learned my job quickly. But I only learned to do the usual household chores. One day she said, 'Saburan, learn to cook. Your wages will go up and you'll always find a job wherever you go in this town.' But who was going to teach me? My mistress said to the middle-aged woman who cooked for her, 'Teach her a bit of cooking. It'll make your work lighter, you'll get some rest once in a while, and when you fall ill, she should be able to manage.' The cook woman was my mother's age but full of envy. She thought the mistress was planning to get rid of her. She didn't teach me much, but I watched her when she cooked to see how much salt or oil you needed in what and what needed frying and for how long. My mistress loved me as I stayed close to her. I got things done even before she had opened her mouth, as if it was my own house. She was very pleased with me and the cook. She bought us a set of clothes for Eid. My sari cost a little more than the cook's and that she couldn't bear. When there was a need for quality cookery, my mistress took charge of the kitchen herself. She was not only a good person, she was a good cook. 'Saburan,' she used to tell me, 'watch me cook.' I used to follow her methods carefully. It's not hard to learn when you've got someone like her to teach you. The real thing is love, which can change life; it's not just teaching. 'How's your student learning?' my mistress would ask the cook. 'Let her cook one or two things once in a while.' The cook couldn't disobey the mistress, so I took the exam and passed well. I cooked a vegetable dish or something, I can't remember, but I remember my mistress's encouragement. I learned to cook a few dishes. I don't think I could ever cook them on my own income, but there was no harm learning. I learned to cook biriani, chicken mussallam, and such like due to the memsahib's kindness. Yet I had to leave within a year. Meanwhile my wages had gone up. Chacha used to come and collect it when my mistress had her afternoon nap. I gained the courage to go out a little on my own. My mistress approved and said I should know a bit of the surroundings as people became stupid if they got confined in their homes. To me this town was no longer a python which would swallow me whole as I'd thought earlier. I changed many houses after that. I sometimes got the sack for nothing. You couldn't tell what some of these idle mistresses would do next. I was a working woman and I kept fit, but disease lay siege to them. One of my mistresses burned with jealousy. She often lay bedridden, visited by doctors. Lying in bed, she thought the master was admiring the firmness of my body. Mother of three or four, but look at her. She thought I was seducing her man. The rich eat a variety of things, they don't work, Allah knows who and what tickles them and where. If you're tickled under the armpit you laugh; if you're tickled elsewhere, you get aroused. It didn't take me long to realise that the memsahib either envied or suspected me. Besides cooking, I used to run errands in that house. If I took a glass of water to the master, who at the moment might have been reading a letter, he'd finish reading it before he drank the water. So when I returned with the glass, the mistress would ask: 'What were you doing in sahib's room?' Her insinuations set me on fire. She was my mistress, but just listen to her. 'Why does the master call you so often?' Now answer that. Could you work in a house like that? Then in another house I lost my honour. Thanks to Allah, I found Qazi. Allah found him for me. So many things come rushing to my mind I can't grasp them all. I quit that job because I knew I could find another. As long as the city kept growing, there would be no end of jobs. A growing city meant that the number of rich people went up too. They needed people to work for them. I used to make enquiries through domestics. I used to go out on my own as I was not scared of doing so any more. There were usually many people in the streets. Ten or twenty would come running to your rescue if you screamed. Fear of what? Even on my own, I'd once gone out after the sahibs had eaten their lunch. Not many people lived in these exclusive areas, where houses were built in spacious grounds. Neighbours didn't mingle much at all. With no workshops or bazaars, there were very few people in the streets. I'd hardly walked for four or five minutes before I saw these youngsters coming out of a large gate. They had tight jeans on. They whistled as they walked behind me. I pretended I hadn't heard. They lived in the area and had clean clothes on. I shouldn't be annoyed if they whistled. They hadn't as yet betrayed any bad intention. But when they kept whistling and making rude noises with their tongues and lips, I couldn't keep my cool. There wasn't anyone else in the street. People were having their afternoon naps after lunch. But I didn't tremble. I turned round. No sooner had one of them put his hand to his mouth to make a rude noise than an angry, 'Aren't you sons of gentlemen?' shot out of my mouth. They stopped, probably taken aback, for they'd no immediate answers. Then raising their voices they said, 'So what?' 'Don't you understand, sons of gentlemen though you are?' One, who would give you the creeps the way he groomed his hair and moustache, said, 'No, we don't understand.' I don't know what happened to me, but I too raised my voice. 'Don't you?' I said. 'Go home and do that to your sister and she'll tell you.' A car was coming in that direction. 'I'll scream now,' I said, 'if you don't stop walking behind me.' I was really angry. Did I have to honour them just because they were children of good homes? Well, their behaviour was loutish. They disappeared into a side street. The car passed me slowly. From his clothes I realised the driver was not a chauffeur, but the owner of the car himself. As he passed, he looked me up and down and then drove away whistling. I liked that, I mean being looked at. I didn't see the youngsters any more. They were being rude, or I wouldn't have bothered. I felt if I'd chosen to come out on my own, I shouldn't mind if someone enjoyed looking at me, but my body wasn't so public that I'd let them get away with rudeness. I had courage then. Now I feel lonely and I've lost my way. Qazi got arrested. You can trust him, but he's in trouble himself. Still, one can depend on Allah. He did once find Qazi for me. Qazi was a godsend, what else can I call him? When he came on the scene, goodbye to domestic service for the sahibs and memsahibs. At least I didn't have to run errands or cook any more. I still did all these things of course, but not as a servant. I used to go to my Chacha's to give him my wages. Sometimes he himself came to collect them. He also gave me news from home. Then one day Allah smiled on me and I earned a lot of money, but my line to Chacha closed and along with that stopped news from home. Good things don't come all at once. If a stream flows in one direction, it dries up in another. 'Allah doesn't offer you everything at once,' Qazi used to say. 'One should grab happiness with both hands when it's given, because once it slips from your hands, only Allah can tell how long it'll be before it comes again.' I took Qazi's sayings as truth. I can't remember them all, but some of them still ring in my ears. 'When you go fishing you get wet and dirty, but when you eat the fish, you're not wading in muddy water. This is the way of the world. If you get dirty, no matter, you can clean yourself later.' Qazi was hard to fathom. He used to visit the sahib I was then working for. There's nothing unusual about people crowding to the houses of big bureaucrats. Everybody knows they've a lot of power. If you can be friendly with one, it might come in handy. You can't tell how things will turn out in the end. It's all Allah's will; we humans can't tell when good times will come for us. My master had four or five children — two of them lived abroad. One, who went to college, was a year or two younger than me. I was a servant and I knew my place. I cooked and occasionally ran errands. The college boy was very shy; he hardly spoke and when he asked for things, he did so in a gentle voice. The two girls talked with their parents, but not the boy. He replied to questions in a word or two and had his dinner quietly without so much as looking up. You'd think butter wouldn't melt in his mouth. He slept in a room of his own. The servants slept in their room across the courtyard. They retired to their rooms after finishing their daily chores and I went to sleep in the kitchen. As I was the only female servant in the house, the mistress had made this arrangement for me. There was a window in the kitchen but hardly any air came through it. So when it was hot I kept the door ajar. One hot night I'd fallen asleep, leaving the door open. Suddenly I realised that someone lay on top of me holding me in a tight grip. I didn't know what to do. Should I scream? My mouth was under arrest, overblown by the stranger's hot breath. The man had the strength of a tiger. I couldn't move. The room was dark and the man had penetrated my darkness so fast there was nothing I could do. Things had happened so fast. As he got off me, he whispered, 'Don't tell anybody. Here's one hundred taka for you.' Before going, he touched my lips with his hot lips. I knew from the voice that he was the young master, the quiet devil. He wasn't a boy; he was a woman eater. I lay there in silence; I was angry. But what could I do? First I thought I'd tell the memsahib. Then I thought I'd tell the girls. For two days my mind was in turmoil. Should I leave? The quiet devil behaved as if nothing had happened. He came to the table for his meals and returned to his room without a word. I was disgusted with myself. Finally I decided to tell the memsahib. Other maids who'd come to work here would then be safe. If I'd lost my honour others needn't. A couple of days later after lunch I stood hesitantly at the memsahib's door. It wasn't easy. It'd have been easier if it were not about her son. With my eyes and ears shut, I told her everything in one breath. Only I didn't mention the money, though I had the one hundred taka in my fist. I thought I'd throw it away in front of her, but I couldn't. The memsahib looked quiet and grave for a while and then said, 'You may go now. I'll see to it. Don't tell anybody.' I'd heard the same words the other night and made a hundred taka and the money was still in my fist. The following morning the young master didn't come to the table. I went about my usual chores but I wasn't myself. After breakfast the Memsahib called me into her room.

She shut the door herself, didn't ask me to do it. I won't lie now, I was scared. What was she going to do? First she gave me a lecture. Not in a loud voice. It was my fault if something had happened, she said. Her suckling child couldn't possibly do anything of the kind. Well, who had opened the door? She was annoyed when I told her that I did it because it was hot but did not raise her voice lest she should be heard outside the door. But her poison had the virulence of a cobra's. The heat, she said, was inside me, not out there. I lowered my head and listened to her. She opened the almirah and took out some money to pay me off. 'You're fired,' she said. Usually you ask to stay for a day or two to find a new job, but I knew I couldn't stay there a moment longer. That butcher of a woman had given me a sari on the Eid day. I had it on me at the time. She asked me to take it off before leaving. There wasn't much difference between mother and son; both took other people's clothes off. I packed and went to the sahib to take leave. He was in the sitting room, talking to friends. He was surprised when I said goodbye. He wanted to know what had happened. The mèmsahib had fired me, I said. Did I have a job to go to? No. Qazi, whom I'd seen there before, was sitting there. 'I need someone to work for me,' he said. 'Then take her, if she'll go.' I thought I'd grasped the moon. I didn't hesitate when I was asked. I got the job right then. I didn't want to haggle over my wages. I might end up having to go back to Chacha, and I was loath to go back to that hell. I thanked Allah for his kindness. Qazi drove me home. He asked me a lot of questions then. I don't know why I told him so much. We'd only just been introduced, it wasn't normal to be so open. But I didn't feel he was a man to be wary of. Where did he live and with whom, did he have a family — these are some of the questions one should ask before taking a job. My first mistress told me, 'Saburan, it's a hell of a problem being born a woman in this country.' I remembered these words as I sat in the car and saluted that sympathetic soul, not by raising my hand, you understand. I'd travelled by bus before, but I'd never had the chance to ride in a car. I looked about at the city as the cool breeze soothed my body. Rows of buildings, people and the traffic. I wondered where I was going and with whom, but I was not daunted by the thought. My life in town had at least given me that much confidence. If I was going to be battered by life, that was my destiny, but I wanted to see it through. At times I felt empty inside, but I also had a feeling of strength coming from somewhere. Qazi drove me around for a long time, about two or three hours. 'Let me tell you this,' he once said, but did not. I was a little apprehensive. If I was only supposed to work as a domestic servant, why was I being made such a fuss of? 'You won't be required to cook at my place,' he said as he drove. 'There are others for that. You'll do as I tell you and look after others.' 'It's one's duty to do that anyway,' I said. Qazi was pleased. 'You're a clever girl,' he said. It was my turn to be pleased. I spent three years at his place. He knew I could do a job when I was given one. The car went a long way along a narrow lane and turned into more lanes to the right and to the left. Then we came up to this three storeyed building behind an iron gate, covered with iron plates. When the gate was shut you wouldn't see much of the building. Qazi had stopped the car to buy one or two saris for me. 'Put them in your bag,' he said. He'd also bought a cloth bag for me. 'You'll need them.' I was apprehensive, but didn't panic.

He took me to the second floor of the building and said, 'This is your room.' Room? Cooks usually sleep in the kitchen. What was all this? There was a proper bed, all made, with a mosquito curtain. Sometimes sahibs give you a mosquito net, sometimes not. I'd often been tormented by mosquitoes. 'Where's your family, sir?' I asked Qazi. 'They don't live here. Some relations do.' I was scared now. I looked at his face. Perhaps he guessed I was scared. 'Don't be afraid,' he said. 'There are other girls. You'll have company.' 'Who are they?' 'They're my people. I'll tell you what. Put away your old clothes in that almirah and put on one of your new saris. And take this key. This is for you, don't give it to others. There are towels in the bathroom. Have a wash. I'll tell Subeda about your dinner.' When Qazi left I had a wash. When I was shedding my skin, a girl of my age walked in. Slim and good-natured by the look of her. She introduced herself. Her name was Subeda. 'And yours?' 'Saburan, but call me what you like. Are you a relative? Are you from his village?' Then I made other queries. 'Where's the kitchen?' 'We do the cooking. You're new here, you don't have to go to the kitchen today. Have a rest.' 'Where's Qazi sahib?' 'He's gone out. He'll be back. He's a busy man.' 'Are there no males in this house?' 'No end of them,' Subeda said. 'They're busy. They come when they want to. You don't have to worry about them.' That was how my first day there started. Qazi returned to see me later. 'Give me your home address,' he said. 'I'll see to it that your father gets two hundred taka each month.' Two hundred taka! It was a surprise. O destiny, I thought, was I going to be of so much use to my father? I'd left the one hundred taka note the young master gave me under a tin of spices in the kitchen. Was I to take that devil's money? Now here I was being offered two hundred taka a month. Well, I thought, Allah will be kind to you if you are honest. But the way is not straight, there are many twists and turns. I was trapped. Two hundred taka was not to be sniffed at. Though I had to go to the kitchen every day I was freed from the monotony of cooking. My way of life changed, and with it my menu. Fish and meat every day; in the past it depended on the kindness of the mistress. Only my first mistress was different; she gave a little bit of something to everybody, however little. The piece of meat could be small, but meat there would be. And fish when there was fish. My other mistresses — it wouldn't be too much to call them whores. Suppose they invited people to dinner, had five or six guests — such food! The servants still got the same miserable stuff. Now I had everything in my control. I could even get a little milk. Qazi often bought sweets for us. I bought them too when I went out. Within a matter of months I'd become a 'partner' in Qazi's business. Qazi affectionately called me partner. I was helpful to him. A lot of people visited that house, all gentlemen. They were looking for pleasure. Some wanted company when they were in town. Qazi gave me strength; well, perhaps not quite that. But how could I forget that I was now able to help Bap? Once I had felt contempt for the offer of a hundred taka note; had felt centipedes were walking all over me. Now, a few months later, nothing seemed to matter any more. Now I picked up the centipedes from the drain and let them crawl all over me. There was a lot of money in it. It all depended on how rich the centipedes were of course. Qazi didn't live in that house, but he dropped in every day for days and then disappeared for five or six. He'd then say, 'Partner, take care.

There's the gateman. Don't go out for a few days now.' I didn't know everything about Qazi. People visited the house, but he didn't bring them along. They came on their own. Qazi had forbidden me to talk too much to people I didn't know. When someone dropped in, everybody knew why he'd come, and when their needs were satisfied they left. The women in the house cooked for themselves. There were two female cleaners. One of them washed dishes in the morning and the other swept and cleaned the house. They were *adibasi* untouchables. As they'd lived here for a long time, they spoke a little Bangla. They were paid well, so they were happy. Qazi had advised me to buy some gold jewellery as cash wouldn't keep. He said he'd himself buy some for me. Of late he'd been saying, 'Partner, I'll wind up the business. But don't panic. I'm saving your money for you. You'll get what you want. A bit of land in your village so that your father doesn't starve in his old age, that's all you want, isn't it? By the will of Allah, you'll have it. I, too, got into the business — well, I'll tell you the story another day.' But he never did. He raised me from the level of a slave girl and offered me the pleasures of a lady. If he didn't want to tell me about his past, well and good, I didn't want to pester him. Many women came to that house. Some came in the evening and disappeared in the morning. Some stayed for three or four months. I knew Qazi's men found jobs for them. Subeda was a good girl; one day she too went away. 'Where are they going to send you?' she asked me. 'Qazi sahib knows that,' I said. But later Qazi snapped at me, 'Leave it to me. I'll decide if you want a job or what. You don't have to worry about it.' It's not that I didn't disapprove of my way of life now and then, but you get used to it if you're under pressure. I had to provide pleasure to some special friends of Qazi. Of late I hardly recognised myself when I stood before the bedroom mirror. Clothes and good looks apart, good food, as I'd realised from my experience with my mistresses, gave you a good figure. I'd got used to that life. Qazi told me he wouldn't stay in the business too long. We had open and frank talks, but strange man! He just came to talk to me. Only once did he gently shake me by the chin. 'There's Allah,' he said. 'Allah will fulfil your needs.' He didn't show any more interest in me than that. I wouldn't have minded a bit of fun now and then. Who cares to be in a straightjacket of rules? Sometimes I felt really low. I'd left home a long time ago. How was Bap? I could remember my youth, one or two girls of my village. Where are they now? Those who'd got married would have had children by now, clinging to them in their miserable homes. I used to think there was no misery so big that a fistful of rice and a few clothes wouldn't take care of it. By rights I should have been happy. But I wasn't. What happened to me? Sometimes I felt so angry I could have burnt the whole city down. Here there was a lot of wealth *and* a lot of sin, while people in the country went without food and quarrelled over scraps. Now that I'd enough to eat I wanted to get back to Bap and friends and acquaintances. I often thought about my husband. Poor man! He might have run away to avoid starting a family. That would've been a burden. But did he ever think about me? He spoke such sweet words in bed to get the better of me, the deceiver. I still remember his face. I even feel a little sorry for him. I had no hint before he went that he was going to disappear. He was a country lad, had a good face, at least I thought so. I've seen so many faces since, swines the lot of them, but polished. I was lucky I didn't have to look at them for long. Now my face has become polished too. I use soap every day and bathe in running water. I remember the village pond. Bap used to tell us off when we, some girls of my age, made the water muddy. In the summer we wouldn't leave the pond once we were in it, we'd stay in as long as possible. Then one day I walked across the fields with Chacha and boarded a boat and a bus to get to the railway station. That was the first time I saw a train. I don't want to see anything any more. I feel like lying down and closing my eyes for months on end. People die. They're lost when they die. They may be lost even before they die. Chacha still lives in the town, but I don't see him. I can only guess how they are. But they're lost and so is Bap. Dark thoughts come to my mind and I'm scared. If Bap's really lost, where shall I go? To whom? And if he's not in the village it'd be pointless going back there. Qazi's still here, but I don't know much about him. Ours was a business relationship. What if that relationship's finished? Things were fine, everything was turning out well. Qazi's an educated man, I'm illiterate, but he treated me as one of his own. It's hard to say who gets what from another. Why should Qazi, an important man, talk to me? I'm ignorant, with not much to say for myself, but Qazi did and he drank cups of tea. What did he have in mind? I was much younger than him. Was that why he didn't consider any other relationship with me? What wouldn't I have given him? But he kept his distance, and came to me just for the company, to talk. Sometimes I was given certain responsibilities. The city lay at my feet. I could travel to any part of it by rickshaw and nobody would've known from my clothes that I was an ignorant country girl. Once upon a time I stumbled as I walked in this town, but for a time I was as free as air, blowing whichever way I pleased. Things were fine and everything was turning out well until — ah, I don't want to think any more — lightning struck. One night the police surrounded the house. I walked in a trance to the police vehicles with two or three girls. I guessed from the conversation of the policemen that Qazi had been arrested in another house, where those who stayed were all men. Their business was sending people abroad. What was wrong with that? In our house there was another business and this was certainly bad. In this country you've got to sign in at a police station to do the business. How big an offence was it to do it without signing in? The police locked up the entire house. The offence couldn't be that small. I heard the policemen saying that Qazi was held in the male cells of the prison. I didn't blink, I just stared into the dark as the police vehicle drove off. Ya Allah, your kindness knows no bounds. What have you done now? I was all right, everything was turning out all right, what have you done now, Kind One? I didn't scream, but my heart was screaming inside me. I want to go back to my father, take me home...Ya Allah...Oh Lord. Here in town you can't hear the cicadas.

CHAPTER TWO

I am Qazi Alamin. I know you won't believe what I have to say. I know people *enjoy* listening to the confessions of a man in prison on criminal charges, but does anybody believe them? But then, why do I need anyone to believe me? I've never had so much rest in my life since I fell into this legal trap, and when the body rests, the mind becomes restless. Of course, as I've discovered to my cost, it's the mind that rests when the body is active, so, after a long time of acting and not thinking, now that I've got time to look at myself, I really need to look back and see how I've got to this present position. I may not be able to get to the end but my mind is on the move. As both speaker and listener, I feel as if I've been cast on a current of silence. Sometimes I scream inside myself and perhaps this causes some kind of vibration somewhere, but I don't know. As a human being I need someone. One seeks a neighbour. What else is the sweetheart of a *baul* singer? I don't want just one neighbour, I want many, many people. I've been looking for them since my consciousness awoke, but haven't as yet found myself a permanent home. I found 'neighbours' but the hope of living with them kept receding; a mirage on the horizon, true only in dream. I changed tack, I thought, let's have an experiment. For experiments to be successful, you need research, but, shackled to the iron chains of life, a man is not in control in his laboratory. I'm fifty, now. I was an adolescent when Pakistan was created. Whatever I've done since my youth I've done in order to earn a living, which means I haven't had the opportunity to make experiments with my life. My parents died when I was young. I was supported by my uncle. I was not a good student, I knew I had no brains. Who could I compete with? Cut your coat according to your cloth, as they say. In the fierce currents of social competition, many are swept away. I was cautious, I didn't want anything big. The imagination of a lower middle-class child remains limited right from the start. It's all fixed for you. A bit of schooling, followed by a life free from the most nagging wants of life. I was born in the country, where fields stretched far but imagination was bounded. I'm not ashamed to admit that my aspirations were limited. My mind was under the spell of the country. Even after I'd spent two years in a provincial town reading for a degree, I still didn't realise that the city was the best arena for the struggle to survive. My family stayed on in the country while I moved on to the city. They now live in a small provincial town, have done so for the last six or seven years. They had to leave my village home for various reasons. Four people make up my family; two daughters and a son, besides the wife. When I started on the business, keeping in touch with them was difficult. Before that I only had a clerical job. I spent twenty years in it. During that period, I had a routine of contact with the family. Fifty or sixty miles from the city, the place was three hours journey by train. You could set off on Saturday and return on Sunday. I couldn't really afford the luxury of spending so much money just for a day — it was different when I had a holiday of two or three days at a time — yet whenever I felt a great urge for the pleasures of the clan I would set off on Saturday. I enjoyed playing with the wife and children, but I had to pay for it afterwards. The misery of my city life increased. I could hardly cut down on my boarding charges. I'd much rather have suffered personal hardships than be humiliated in front of the three other people I lived with. But what when there was no alternative? My bouts of pleasure would land me on a bed of nails. It meant borrowing from messmates and colleagues. Besides, I'd have had to stop caring about my health and sacrifice my little yearnings for years on end. I couldn't hope to bring the family to live with me in the city. I didn't have many friends then, I was something of a recluse. But it would be hard for someone from my past to recognise me today. The sleeping snake raises its hood when it's disturbed. This is what happened to me. Flood water breaks down dikes, but how many notice the secret cracks which have been menacing them long before. Living in the city with the family was a futile hope. It's not easy to sympathise with other people's suffering. Classes live within their compounds; one's vision doesn't extend beyond the fence of one's class. There are further limitations. There are cubicles within the same compound; someone occupying one cubicle is not likely to know what's happening to those in the other cubicles. Imagine you go home on a long holiday of seven or eight days such as you'd take for *Eid*. If your wife is having her period or suffering from lucorrhea, she's definitely out of bounds for ten days. Can you save up the pleasures of a holiday to be enjoyed later? Occasional cough and cold apart, Allah be praised, I enjoyed good health. But the children endlessly suffered from one thing or another, and there was no money for treatment. The end-of-month letters from the wife were usually so crammed with such news that I often considered becoming a fakir and abandoning the world. Sometimes I had to go home on official leave with borrowed money in my pocket. My poor wife was overworked. She was once pretty; a shadow had now spread over her fair skin. I felt sorry for her, pitied her, but such impotent pity and sorrow were no use to anybody. I cried at the court of Allah, but my days never brightened. My wife had a modest ambition; she wanted us to live together in the city. She worried about me living on my own. Cooks were not easily found in the city so we messmates had to make do with whatever we could cook. This made the wife anxious, so I stopped telling her about my difficulties. Not on top of the troubles she had with the children! If only they'd had the benefit of good education, perhaps the good lord would look kindly on us in our old age. But this was not to happen. I was fourteen when the country was partitioned. I'd gone on political demos and split the sky with shouts of *Pakistan Zindabad, Quide Azam Zindabad*. Our elders used to say that the English and their allies, the Hindus, were responsible for the misfortunes of the Muslims of India. The Hindus dominated all spheres of life, so the Muslims needed a homeland. Then Allah got us Pakistan. But our troubles didn't go away. The influential Hindus, the cause of our fears, were there no more. I was in the first year in college in nineteen fifty when the rich Hindus left the country following a religious riot, and those who stayed were keeping their heads down. Why then did the condition of the Muslim remain unchanged? At the time I thought this was natural in a new state. The Muslim League government talked a lot about the 'infant' state. The name was appropriate, but the infant didn't grow, being crippled at birth. Now I ask questions, but at the time I didn't look into things in any depth. I was busy reading for my exams, and keeping your head stuck in a book was endlessly pushed as a student's one great duty. I didn't rack my head over these questions even when I'd found a job. Allah provides and there's nothing one can do about divine dispensation. My family was pious. I can't remember my father, but my uncle never missed a prayer. Then there was my childhood teacher, a moulvi, a man of piety. He used to tell us that Allah was kind to those who lived honestly. The moulvi was a handsome man; even more admirable was his melodious voice. His recitation of the Holy Quran was well worth listening to. His influence on me was not in vain; the thickly grown beard you can see on my face is only seventeen or eighteen years younger than me. I don't think I've ever shaved my beard. Do your duty, Allah says, but why does one suffer for all one's honesty? While many suffer, a few who don't bother to follow Allah's instructions get on very well in the world. 'The voice of the people is the voice of God,' I've heard from the lips of elders, of teachers, since childhood. But even if He stays with the majority they don't escape the hammer of want. Only a handful have all the fun. Whose side is Allah on? Does He perhaps test the pious with suffering? If one looks at a thousand years' history, the conclusions come massing in rows. It seems that a handful of people enjoy the gifts of Allah while others don't even question the way things go. How does that happen? Are people deceived? Doesn't the deception ever get exposed? I started asking these questions later in life and I didn't get any honest answers. I'm a quiet man; arguing with people is against my nature. But I couldn't get away from myself. I felt worse when I saw that some of my colleagues didn't suffer as much as I did. Four of us had rented a large room with an attached bath. The condition of one of them was similar to mine. The third colleague was a little better off as his father had left him a bit of land from which he received enough rice to see him through the year. The last one, Ramiz Ali, left us after a few years to live with his family in the city. It's a sin to talk behind people's backs so I didn't comment on his conduct. But my two colleagues spared nobody. 'Crawled to the bosses.' 'It's the unlawful earnings which have the most *barkat*.' 'Shameless swine, we've lived together for all these years. Now that you've left us to shack up with your family, shouldn't you invite us at least once for a meal?' I didn't take part in these discussions, but I overheard them. If you live together you can't keep your ears shut. One day I said, 'Why talk about him? Besides, we shouldn't accept even a cup of tea there, for things at the house of someone who's violated the law are unlawful.' But my colleagues wouldn't be silenced. One of them seemed unable to digest his food unless he could puff away while making disparaging remarks about our old colleague. He was otherwise an honest man. His only other fault was that he smoked *bidis*. I never picked up that habit but when I started on this business I soon learned that you had to carry cigarettes on you. I also realised why people spent thousands on cigarette advertisements. I used to offer cigarettes to my business associates. Every business has its own rules. There were certain things I knew I had to do; if you register yourself as a prostitute you can't choose between fat and thin. Sometimes I had no option but to smoke, just make-believe. If I offered someone a cigarette, he'd probably say, 'And you?' to which I'd say, 'I don't usually smoke, it's not a habit. I just had a packet on me, I'll smoke one later.' If I didn't have to, I really wouldn't go anywhere near them. I've met all sorts of people in business. I knew one who wouldn't do anything without a bottle. It's all give and take in business. Can you just take without giving? There's nothing one-sided in this world. But, by Allah,

I've kept off the forbidden drink. 'I've had an abscess of the liver,' I used to say, 'I have to obey the doctor's orders.' Would any gentleman insist after that? When I got into this business, I soon found out that there's no guile a bad sort lacks. But I had to supply drinks and I've never asked any *fatwa* dispenser if, like bribes, both the taking and the giving of drinks were forbidden in Islam. If someone was desperately looking for a drinking partner, he'd be put out if he couldn't find one. So I used to join in with a glass of soft drink like sherbet or soda water... Saburan, a country girl whom I remade. She climbed all the steps so easily. I should have given her some education, though; she could have been even more useful. A gem of a girl, very self-possessed. She fitted in. She sacrificed much to make a living. In particular circumstances, one doesn't take long to shed one's skin. Trousers, Hawaiian shirts, suits — I'd never dreamed I'd wear so many types of clothes. But if you're in business, you change clothes according to the weather. Can you wear muslin in the Himalayas? They say there are seven layers of heaven. It's the same on earth. Each class has its own way — conversations, behaviour, its sense of humour. There's bantering at every level, but every level has its own way of doing it. If you don't understand that, you'll soon be put in your place. At first I used to sit around mutely. Then I learned the ropes and joined in the laughter — though not always spontaneously. Suppose someone wants to get a job done — a party is arranged and, of course, there's no point to it without the patron, and if you can't light up a little self-esteem in him, you'll go bankrupt. Your very existence, your future, are tied to the success of your business. So you've got to have a tactic, a strategy. When the patron tells a joke, you have to laugh loudly enough to split the sky the moment the story ends, laughter so long and violent your friends begin to worry they might have to take you to a doctor to sew up your guts. You have to pretend that, until then, the source of such profound, perpetual laughter hadn't been discovered. How long it takes you to learn such a skill depends, of course, on your intelligence. It didn't take me long. I often wonder how I'd lived so passively for so long. Perhaps my intelligence was hibernating. Then I met Saburan. She was waiting for the chance to do something with her life. All she wanted was someone to show her the way. In the beginning I had some misgivings. She was someone else's daughter and so young; should I be pushing her into sin? My own daughter will be sixteen soon. She's the oldest of my three children. But you can't ignore the ways of business. Saburan's a clever girl, she took the hint smartly enough. Now it's clear to me that your moral duties don't extend beyond your own little world. All honest men know that they should help other people in distress. But who are these other people? Relatives, acquaintances? Aren't there others beyond them? If you're a good man, the misery of your relatives or neighbours will disturb you. But there are others beyond them whom you don't know, who exist for you only as a vague abstraction. You don't feel you have any responsibility towards them. All you care is that your daughter or of someone close to you doesn't go astray or live by selling her body. In this country, the sphere within which moral duties reign is very small indeed. Saburan found me in a dilemma. But, when it comes down to it, it's business which matters. You just can't deny its demands. You live in the middle of fierce competition where it's fatal to become a saint. You'll soon find yourself ostracised—and what's more, they'll not only ostracise you, they'll destroy you, as you could endanger their existence.

Many honest men in this country are blind in this way. Perhaps I shouldn't say blind, it's just that they suffer from tunnel vision. Like a surgeon who plies his knife on his patient but doesn't consider himself a murderer as he thinks he can foresee the consequences of his action, I pushed Saburan on to the murky road, letting the kite fly but still holding the string in my hand. Those who live in desperate want see in the satisfaction of that want the road to salvation. Saburan was no exception. She was eager to take risks to help her destitute father. She was very open and frank with me and I pitied her. I learned how she'd lost her last job. Having been married and then raped, she was physically experienced. Let her pick up some more experiences, I thought. It needn't have to be for long or very often. If you give supreme importance to filling an empty belly, you'll find a reason for anything. Saburan was no exception. How could she reject the possibility of helping her father to a level that even the parent of three or four couldn't hope for? In our line of business it's better not to have a permanent address. Saburan had accepted this arrangement. Her father didn't know her address; arrangements were made for him to receive some money. A man was entrusted with the job. The same method is followed to get the city newspapers to their subscribers. We had a complete network in the city for our communications. Now, inside prison, I can see myself more clearly and transparently. I realise that beneath the calm surface of my past life, unknown to me, fermentation must have been going on. How else could I change so quickly? There must have been a knot somewhere in that tangled web which I'd overlooked. Or why should it turn out as it did? All's well that ends well, goes the old adage. My future is uncertain. Between the larger teeth of the saw there are small ones. There are those who are above me, who do not get their hands dirty. They have an advantage over us; they can get away with it. The law is their patron. But if they don't shield me, they too might get trapped in the end, and that's my only hope. When the police take me to court, my patrons are sure to fight my legal battle. They'll have to employ big lawyers on my behalf. I wasn't in touch with them all, but one or two will certainly come to the court with their friends and pay large fees from the wings. I hear Saburan couldn't withstand police interrogation; she's named names. But then most of those she's named have more than one address. The police may find that while the cage is there, the bird has flown. Even if they find any, they should know how to escape. Besides, the police know there are large teeth over small ones. Saburan knows a few people and a few houses. She knows some names but she's not likely to remember their addresses. Though clever, she's still illiterate — and, many people don't realise, there are advantages in working with the illiterate. Lawyers' cross-examination will reveal many gaps in the law. The real question is not one of truth or falsehood, right or wrong. Lawyers take fees to get their clients off the hook. If they lose, they lose their good name; they get more clients if they win. But that's where my fears begin. I haven't got any savings. What money I made I used to buy either jewellery or bits of land in the name of my wife and children. None of these made any visible change in our way of life. My wife was happy with my prosperity, but her hope of our living together could not be realised. Poor thing, she'd suffered so much. By the time Allah looked kindly at us, the other thing had emptied out and my desire for her company diminished. I still don't desire other women, perhaps due to age-old prejudices. My daughters and my sons are the apples of my eye. Even in the middle of a thousand preoccupations, my separation from them makes me sad and I lose my natural good humour. I worked like an addict to make money, leaving no time for anything else. I wonder where the final curtain will find me. I've often prayed to the good Lord and perhaps it was his will that I take another road. But if I didn't have any peace in the past, I still haven't any. Ten years is a long time but it has the insubstantiality of a dream. Sometimes I paint a very dark picture of my future. What if I get gaoled for ten years? All my hard work would amount to nothing. All's well that ends well. Financial security, a life of leisure, winning a seat of honour in the eyes of one's neighbours — there's nothing more an ordinary man can want. But everything seems to have gone wrong. My only consolation is that my children won't suffer. My wife has suffered a lot, she's had no time for herself she's been so busy looking after the children. Still, with the jewellery she's got, she'll have no worry on that score. No big dream is likely to seize her. Wealth itself can't make you luxuriate in life. You need mental preparation for that, a mental framework. She was born in a poor home in the country. If you have no vision to start with, you're not likely to dream big. Thanks to Allah, I've seen much, but still I'm timid in imagination. Saburan wants to return to her village home where she spent her childhood and live with her father. My limit is a provincial town. I was actually making arrangements to wind up the business. But though I wanted to wind up quickly, it wasn't possible. Once you've joined a gang, wriggling out of it takes the skills of an escapologist. What happens to the wounded in an abortive raid? You can't keep pace; even if you can walk you can't keep pace. And your greatest enemy is the blood that drips from your wound. Wherever you go, your destination is marked by your dripping blood. Your comrades won't accept you as their friend for all weathers. Longtime relationships, old favours, are wiped out in an instant. You'll even cease to be your own friend. When your face becomes your enemy, your companions will, without a word of regret, sever your head from your body. Otherwise the chain linking faces to people will become an instrument to haul in the whole gang. So be prepared for death, brutal death. I never used to think about these things. I should have. I should have known better. I should have thought about the possible consequences. It's too late now, pointless to regret. It's hard to think of the sand banks when you let yourself go with the current. Then, when the lava erupted, the heat had been trapped for so long it was absurd to think of trying to stop its flow with your hands. Instead you think: let things drift. They'll find their own solution. There was a time when I used to feel tired all the time, fell asleep after office hours and sometimes slept until after sunset. I used to sleep through the time for evening prayer. I felt guilty about it for a time, then stopped bothering; I became defiant: I haven't said my prayers: so what! The guilt had gone. One day, back home after the office, I found a letter from home. My wife, in her childish hand, had written asking me to go home. All the children had fallen ill simultaneously. What with nursing the sick, cooking and the household chores, she wasn't coping. Neighbours couldn't be expected to come and sit around for so long. People had work to do. Fortunately, they had lent money, though even on that count things weren't easy. There weren't any rich folk around. Even if there were, who would open a charity home? I put the letter down and fell asleep until after the time of the evening prayer. Perhaps I'd have slept longer. A messmate woke me up. 'What's the matter? Are you ill?' 'No, just tired,' I said, 'I've no strength left after the office.' I just couldn't make myself get up, though the letter charged through my brain. I had to borrow some money. In my imagination I paraded some of the people I knew. I wasn't good at making friends. Some people are witty, some tell jokes. I had nothing to offer on those counts. I was a real introvert then. In time I learnt to fly with the birds, but here in prison I've returned to my old habit of swimming inside my own self. There are other prisoners, but my talk with them is strictly formal. I don't want to know what they've done. If someone comes to talk, wanting to get a load off his chest, he's discouraged by my inattentive monosyllables. Within a few days, my fellow prisoners realised that, though I moved about, I was a mute stone. A 'No Entry' sign hung over my sombre face and my luxuriant beard. I'd inherited a good physique. I wasn't short, had muscular arms and a wide chest. That's why hardship had never really affected my body. I tried to think of people who could help me in my trouble. I went to see some of them the following morning, but no luck. Financially, they were in the same position as me. Then, hope against hope, I decided to see my old messmate, Ramiz Ali. I had my misgivings. Although a colleague, he was corrupt. But the picture of home kept invading my mind. Ramiz didn't just give me money, he showed me such sympathy that even to have once thought that the man was bad seemed a crime. You get to know a man when you're down. I was rescued from my immediate trouble. Afterwards I was angry with myself. What right had I to indulge my conscience with a wife and children to support? I was responsible for bringing them up. How could I shirk my responsibilities?

Conscience was self-indulgence. If I had some inner misgivings or hesitations, I couldn't possibly care for others. There were some opportunities for extra income at work. I didn't fail to make use of them, but I'd been starving for so long, my hunger seemed to be overwhelming. And by then I'd learned what route to follow. There was no change in my behaviour. I spent my extra earnings on children's clothes or on my own meagre needs. But I'd been shown the way and my greed could no longer be confined within narrow limits. It was like a game of snakes and ladders. When you had luck you went up the ladder. I knew there were snakes in the game. My heart sometimes thumped away so fast it seemed it would stop any moment. But should one stop living because of fear? Soon I discovered the mystery of life in the mouth of the snake. If the game went on, I knew I could probably move from the tail of the snake to find a ladder again. The trouble is that the present snake is a very long one and I haven't reached its tail yet. Maybe this descent will last the rest of my life. When I moved from one ladder to the next waiting at my feet, I didn't think about these things. In a few years time I moved far from the bottom rung. I wasn't a clerk any more. I left my job as well as the area where I lived. My hand-to-mouth existence came to an end. Allah knows where my mute tongue found the strength to leap along like a spring. Security is a magical remedy. When you're freed from the thought of the next meal you can accomplish much. I became a different man after I started on the business. The world is a strange place. Like a mountain it has many layers. One leading uphill has no connection with the layers below. All in one mountain, yet the layers are without any real link. If you move house, you don't bump into old acquaintances, and if you do you straightaway conclude your chance meeting with farewells. You may feel so buoyant that you think you're a soaring balloon and the people down there are looking up to you. I didn't go back to my office after I'd resigned. Ramiz Ali once went to my old mess to look me up. He was a small-timer, happy with tit-bits. He wasn't for all or nothing. He hadn't resigned from his clerical job; he lacked my nerve to make a clean break. Then there's the question of opportunities. Fortune doesn't open up equally to all. I went to see Ramiz Ali with a wristwatch for him, material for a shirt and other such small gifts. My good looks, spotlessly clean clothes and my elegant moccasins must have amazed him. He didn't know how to welcome me in his small house in the old alley. I put him at ease. 'I won't have anything except a cup of tea,' I said. 'Doctor's orders. What you see is an empty shell, stout and healthy in appearance only. Then one has to think of one's age.' Ramiz Ali was pleased, pleased that I'd done well enough to give up the job and start my business. When the question of the nature of my business cropped up, I could talk of export and import in general terms. He didn't want to know what we exported or imported. On my eloquence, he commented, 'I didn't know you could talk so.' 'The demands of business,' I said. 'You sell words before you sell goods, you know.' This was true. Ramiz was equally pleased and embarrassed by the gifts I'd brought. Looking humble, he said. 'That you've remembered me is my good fortune.' 'Remember you?' I said. 'I'll remember you till the day of judgment. You saved me and my children when I was hard up.' 'Please don't mention it. It was all Allah's Wish; what can a man like me do?' I took out two hundred taka from my pocket and said, 'I'm not paying old debts. This is to buy sweets for your children.' I forced the notes into his fist. He asked me my address. 'I'm moving house within a week,' I said. 'I'll send you the address as soon as I move.' I've not seem Ramiz Ali since. For which, of course, there are reasons. There are plenty of similarities between the pickpocket and the robber. Yet they are by no means equal in status. If one were forced to choose between the professions of pickpocket and robber, one would certainly choose to be a robber. The more dangerous to society, the higher up the pecking order — and there's the money. As business grows, more clients are caught in your web. Not only does your workload increase, it also becomes more complex. You tell a hundred lies to suppress one. If the court punishes me, I'll be exiled from normal life for seven or eight years. When I return, the old order to which I belong will be no more. Whatever I've salted away will have been exhausted by then and it will be hard for me to earn a living. My property could be confiscated. Everything rests on Allah; whatever He wills will happen. It'll be enough if my children don't become destitutes. If disaster overwhelms me, I won't be alone. I'll bring others down with me. Saburan is no headache; her testimony won't go far. She doesn't know many people. She knows a few places but that won't do much harm. I gave her minor jobs. 'Give these two passports to so and so and bring me the cheque he gives you.' Saburan's job was to keep the girls who stayed with us for a day or two in good humour and to make sure they didn't get too depressed if they had to stay longer. She obeyed me like a *pir*, absolutely without hesitation. But my best hope lies with those under whose protective umbrella I once moved without fear. They'll arrange lawyers and barristers for me and pull all the right strings. They can't rest until my case is decided one way or the other. I'll of course honour the salt

I've eaten. When I was drifting, their guidance saved me. They knew I could take responsibilities, cope with changing circumstances. It was not all kindness. Fish eaters should remember that the fishermen who catch fish are the ones who get dirty. I knew a few lawyers who advised me on small matters. Obviously arrangements will be made so we don't get hammered by the law. That's why I can sleep. The lawyers will come to see me when the case goes to court, though, of course, I won't get bail. I had my contacts with a few newspapers — for keeping things quiet — or making a sensation of them. When even a crow knows about your movements, the newspapers can make sure that there's no reaction to it now or in the future. We took all sorts of precautions although I didn't personally handle these things — they fell outside my orbit. In such matters it's the larger teeth of the saw who do the cutting, though the small ones aren't without their uses. I was quite friendly with a newspaper reporter. The guts of humans and society are alike. You may not notice any relationship between mouth and bowel, yet they are linked inside the stomach. Big business never ignores the press. They don't employ public relations men for nothing. If there are foreign embassies in your country, they have to be friendly with those too; for they, too, have their reputations to keep. Like guts the world has become intertwined. The tubes spread so far and wide one might go mad looking for their ends. If you want to undo any knots you won't get anywhere, even over two or three years, however hard you try. Our business is not confined within the borders of our country. Import and export extends across the world. Our business has spread likewise, getting tangled in numerous complexities. Newspapers aren't just useful inside the country, their shadows fall across alien lands. One newspaperman was particularly helpful with our foreign links as he was respected in foreign embassies. Unlike love affairs, business relationships are never one-sided. In business there's no unrequited love. The exchanges are immediate, for today nobody's obliged to move physically. One can communicate with the whole world from any obscure corner. Banks, telephone and telex services and clearing agents are all at your beck and call. You can get everything done from your chair. So in business it's meaningless to talk about your country as opposed to other countries, although there may be something to it outside the business arena. My partners have been expanding this business over the years. That's why I can sleep. There's no reason to despair. The worst that can happen is my getting gaoled for ten years, though if that happens, the family will be in real financial trouble. This is where I come up against the wall. One can graze one's knees or sprain one's wrists or ankles trying to scale a wall, but it's useless wishing it wasn't there. You can't expect to get off without injury, but why should you think that the disability of one part will make the whole body useless? I've decided that whatever happens I'll return to the city. Now Saburan is still a simple country girl; she hasn't changed, but I could hardly return to my village home. Could I forsake the herd? There's always the danger that someone might dig up the old crime. Yet time suppresses all, wipes the past from memory. I was hit suddenly. Panic sometimes overcomes me in this suffocating world. I take deep breaths to try to regain mental strength. I don't call upon Allah much any more, though there was a time when I used to attend his court everyday, even when I was in difficulties. Oh, it's dark here. The sound of the sentry's boot approaches and recedes. Sometimes I recall old pictures of homely pleasures. Sometimes, unable to find release from my agony, I feel like screaming out. These last two days my confidence has really sagged. My partners in the wings will become alert when the case goes to court. Whether they stay in the wings depends on me. There lies the difference between the big and small teeth of the saw, though both have bitten through the flesh of the wood. Suicide apart, one can't commit a crime on one's own. Some operate in the foreground of the crime, some stay in the background. Both can get caught and punished, but that tends to depend on those in the foreground. Those in the background will arrange the lawyers and barristers for the case from behind the scene so that I don't panic. I was told this by a fellow prisoner. If you've spread your net far and wide, you'll have many advantages. You can throw dust in the eye of the law. The honour of those in the background depends on me. They'll keep themselves informed of the day-to-day development of the case. They'll monitor its direction. They won't be content with the account in the newspapers, they'll send their own men. Indeed, if the name of someone who is not a defendant crops up in the cross examination, arrangements will be made to see that his name doesn't get into the papers, so his colleagues won't see it. If you haven't got at least that much sense, you won't reach the top of a society where they're all honourable men. They know I could dishonour them. What would they do if my words and behaviour took a certain turn under cross-examination? The big teeth then would reach very low indeed, as low as the small teeth. But the small remains small. If I decided to turn awkward, wouldn't they twist my neck? Perhaps I'm just being paranoid, but many things could happen. However, I'll maintain my professional integrity. I'll think before answering questions in court. I hear that seasoned lawyers, starting with simple questions, lead you into such tortuous thickets of the law that you wouldn't know when you've axed your own foot. My misgivings are not entirely unfounded. I've crossed many fens and jungles in the last ten years. Once a police inspector was asked to fiddle a report, not entirely free of cost. I had the role of negotiator. The poor man threw the book at me and kept his empty hand empty. Perhaps his head was likewise. What was the consequence? He was transferred to an unhealthy outpost. That would have been all right, but he was murdered before leaving for his new post. I don't know who murdered him, for my role was limited to that of briber. The new chief who replaced him was a wise man. It's possible, of course, that his predecessor was murdered for some other reason. But the old incident struck me a few times during the last couple of days. The mind loses its bearings in unusual circumstances. Now and then I'm not just alone, but feel lonely. I've a prosperous and imposing look and I'm middle-aged, so other prisoners steer clear of me after a few words. I don't feel any urge for company either, but worry torments a lonely man. How long will it take the case to go to court? Until it's over, my world's confined to this cell and the yard, and goodbye to rest and comfort. Things are only meaningful when you've got peace of mind. This whole place feels like a jungle of thorns. Here, as outside, night follows day, but it's all meaningless. Sometimes my head starts aching, though I suffer no real physical discomforts here; the jailer and the guards look after my small needs. It's evident that those who were with me for years, to whom I was only the handle of the knife and to whom I clung in my search for a reasonable life, have not quite thrown me to the wolves. This world can be faithless, but even here one has to keep faith at a certain level, or men would have become mere brutes long ago. I'm not alone in this island, but in my heart there's been a landslide. Old faces appear before me, now singly, now all together. My children stand on either side of my wife, nobody smiles. They're still photographs. I travel long distances: adolescence, youth, middle age. Then everything blurs. A large mosaic wall stands before me, now in the brightness of its colours, now in darkness. I stretch my arms to touch it, but then I'm in a still frame too. We're on the opposite banks of a narrow, turbulent river, frozen in mutual gaze. Where did I go wrong? The vague shadows cry: 'The easy road is no road. You wanted happiness for yourself and your family, but you can't live without entanglement in this world.' It seems that the unpleasant truth stops short of opening its mouth to declare itself to me. Where did I go wrong? I was alone, I wanted self-fulfilment. I achieved success step by step. But not everybody can proceed like this. There's a question of opportunity. One can't expect everybody to be deceitful. What would the simple folk do? Must they perpetually rot in life's prison with their pie in the sky? Is my loneliness an atonement for a false step? While one individual may find economic salvation as I did, is it also the road for the millions? It can't be. That's where the mistake is. Where is the way? I crawl with my eyes open, but can't find one. Why not? The sound of the sentry's boot is no answer. I look through the window of the small cell, but solid darkness clangs shut on my brain. The road I considered easy isn't easy. My one-time messmate has become my Imam. I hear that he'll be a witness, tell the court what he knows about my past life. The police got in touch with him. I'll strip him naked if he comes to testify against me. But what do I know about him, apart from a vague surmise that he's good at making money on the side. I haven't seen him doing it. How am I going to prove it? By his lifestyle? Everything gets mixed-up in my head. Oh God, oh Saviour, please send me a little sleep. Sleep, sleep... There's no end to my troubles. The cicadas sing in my ears loudly, very loudly...

CHAPTER THREE

'My lord, the shame and ignominy of the case I now seek to present before you covers the nation like a black shroud. The offence falls in the category of sin. When crime and sin appear hand in hand, the sore appears not only on the exterior of our social life but contaminates the very soul of the nation. Now that the responsibility of presenting the case has, for professional reasons, fallen upon me, I am ashamed of having to put my finger on this putrefying sore. I would have been happier by far if the responsibility had fallen on others.' The deep, penetrating voice of the public prosecutor, Maqbul Ahmed, filled the not-so-large court room.

A few visitors had already taken their seats, in addition to the lawyers of the two sides, the two defendants, the policemen who stood guard over them, and the peons and orderlies. The court room was full. The public prosecutor, usually assisted by one lawyer, had three assistants, and they were by no means all junior men. The defendant was represented by two barristers, Aftab Ali and Mahmud Hossain and their four assistants. The magistrate, Sajed Karim, in a jacket and tie, was in his seat. There were three or four witnesses, men and women.

The public prosecutor continued, his voice laced with emotion. 'Although there is only one defendant, the other, a state witness, not being on the same level as the defendant, one should not weigh the seriousness of the offence by the number of offenders. We will submit the full account, step by step. While the main defendant is one Qazi Alamin, it's obvious he is not alone. The state witness has given us names, but we haven't been able to trace them, as they have abandoned their old addresses to live elsewhere. Regrettably, Qazi Alamin's assistant, Saburan, is illiterate. But it's clear from the police report that she excels any educated lady in native wit. This sin would have been uprooted once and for all if the other offenders were apprehended. But that, as I have already said, is not possible now. Nevertheless, I seek immediate justice for the present defendant, as people of this sort would not hesitate to tarnish the image of the whole country for their selfish ends. Qazi Alamin seems to be a seasoned operator. His net is not confined within the boundaries of this country but extends across the world. Singapore, Malayasia, India, Pakistan, Kuwait, Bahrain, Oman and certain other cities of the Middle East fall within the orbit of this operation.'

The defendant was sitting with his head down, unconcerned. Saburan, though, seemed to be swallowing the words of the public prosecutor. There was no sign of fear on her face, but she looked as if she was surprised to find herself in this strange situation. She was wearing an ordinary, coloured sari and her feet were bare, although she had become quite used to shoes. Perhaps she had forgotten to collect them when she was arrested. She had indeed made a bundle of a couple of saris. This had been suggested to her by the policeman who arrested her, since it was impossible to tell how long she was going to stay in prison. Saburan wondered if her helpless look, and her figure, might have done something to the young policeman.

'Sending people abroad is no offence.' The public prosecutor's voice, now at a low pitch, was still firm. He said that in this shrinking world of modern industry, the demand for labour was strange. Demographic distribution not being even, engineers, doctors and teachers of one country went to another in the interest of their professions. But the defendant had made millions by deceit on the pretext of sending people abroad. The world had certainly shrunk but you couldn't go to any country just because you wanted to. Countries had laws regulating the exits and entries of people. It was an offence not to abide by these laws. You needed passports, visas, permission to obtain foreign currency and such like. The defendant knew it all. 'Yet he has deceived hundreds of people. He has done so in two ways. First, at present, utopia is not Malayasia or Singapore but certain towns in the Middle East where any job is as good as manna. I don't have to explain that these countries in the Middle East, without much contact with the ideas of the civilised world, were long asleep, as were their oil resources.'

At this point, one of the defendant's barristers, Aftab Ali, intoned, 'Objection, my lord.'

The flow stopped. The public prosecutor did not look kindly at his adversary, but his thick glasses concealed his hostility. Magistrate Karim, with his elbows on the desk, lifted his hand, 'Yes, Mr. Aftab.'

'My lord, isn't this history lesson rather irrelevant?'

'Let the public prosecutor continue.'

'When the people of the Middle East woke up, they found that oil was not just oil, it had turned into gold. The whole of the Middle East inflated like a balloon and its people developed the habits of the *nouveaux riches*. They were like starved bedbugs. With fresh dollars in their pockets, they turned their eyes to the glittering prizes to be had from abroad. Prodded by the urge for luxury, they fell headlong into imitating foreign ways. They thought of producing things too, but they had only small populations and their minds had little acquaintance with modern science, so they could not but import people from abroad. There's nothing wrong with that. They had much wealth, so those who worked for them with their hands had a share of it. The eyes of those in the poor countries naturally fell on the Middle East and the agents of the defendant held out great temptations. They made a lot of money by making promises to people, many of whom were not sent abroad at all. It was cheating. They employed another type of deception which was even more heinous. What would you call it but slavery? They exported not just men but women too. These noble spirits brought back female slavery when the civilised world had long freed itself of such a blemish. They enticed country girls away from their homes, often in connivance with their guardians. It can be guessed that they poured out money to this end and the unfortunate souls leaped into shoreless seas with a faith which was fathomless. One could say with one's eyes shut that the main goad was poverty. The dishonour of these unfortunate women began in their own country. It appears from the police report that these women were first brought into the city, then arrangements were made for them to be sent abroad. If the offenders proceeded lawfully, they procured passports, visas, etc. for them; but they also had other methods. During this period the women were not entirely idle. The defendant had rented two or three houses where he put them, and it was his practice to put them to work for, I regret, dishonourable ends. Many so-called honourable men haunted these houses after dark. The police have few doubts about why these people went there, but our witness is unable to confirm this. A few girls were rounded up during the raid, all of whom said they were staying in those houses in the hope of employment. Country girls do not easily admit their dishonour. It can be assumed that these houses had become centres of debauchery. Saburan, who is quite outspoken about the loss of her own honour, cannot speak for anyone else. It seems that she's unwilling to tarnish others with the brush of her own sin. This woman has been with the defendant for years, yet she has no idea why she was not given a job or sent abroad. She told the police that it was all up to the boss and that she had no say in the matter. Anyway, the fact of the matter is that the defendant had started on a business of female slavery. We have reports that not just country girls but some educated women have fallen prey to the temptation. A tendency to believe that there are gold mines in the Middle East and that once you get there all heavenly pleasures will be yours has seized literate and illiterate alike in this country. A letter from an educated girl has unexpectedly fallen into the hands of the police. If necessary it can be read out in the court later. The girl writes that she has many comforts but that the price she pays for them is too high. When a girl writes this sort of thing, it's clear where her pain lies. The defendant has not only been avaricious, he has driven the mothers and sisters of this country to sell their bodies. The stigma attaches not only to those few unfortunate women, but to the whole country.'

The public prosecutor paused for breath. Saburan sat, listening to the lawyer, her head down and eyes hidden. It was hard to say what she really heard, whether, if the sounds entered her ears, she made any sense of them. Qazi Alamin, who had been sitting with his head down from the start, had not lifted it since.

The public prosecutor coughed a little to clear his throat, then resumed in an expansive tone: 'You don't need much imagination to see how these criminal elements — although there is just one of them present — would often get together to plan their deceitful activities. Before sending off these girls abroad, they provided them with a flow of luxuries to harden them so they'd eventually trade in their bodies. If someone from a country hovel has the opportunity to perform their natural functions in a tiled bathroom and choose from an excellent menu of pilau, biriani and assorted fruits, what's she going to think? If fortune shines on me even before I have a job abroad, what great pleasure and happiness must be awaiting me — this kind of thought easily comes to such women, particularly to those who have just come up from the country. Many educated people would let everything go in the face of such temptation — and indeed, many young graduates have lost their everything to these conmen. One cannot help feeling sorry for these unfortunate girls who had much simple faith in the future. I know many—'

Before the public prosecutor could complete his sentence, a loud sob from the witness box put a stop to the flow. Immediately every eye rushed towards its source — a girl sitting beside Saburan. The cry stopped abruptly as the girl fainted. There was a little flurry of movement in the court room. Those near her were encouraged to sprinkle water on her face, to comfort her. About ten minutes passed in this manner until things returned to normal. The public prosecutor grasped the loose end of his speech.

'My lord, many of these young girls have not been able to go abroad. A healthy young woman, regardless of her looks, is much more tempting than a sickly beauty, particularly to those who, for a few hours of pleasure, want to sleep with all the women of the world. These unfortunate women are then cast aside like a lecher's used condoms , as you'll hear from the lips of the witnesses. These things have also been detailed in the police report. It's sad that we can no longer hide our shame from the rest of the world. Now I'd like to produce some more facts about the conspiratorial network these people had set up. I'm deliberately taking so much time to highlight one matter because it's important that the people and the court as their representative appreciate the seriousness of the crimes, nay sins, committed by these criminals. Let us look at one of their many foul activities. Generally you need a certificate to send a person abroad, commonly known as NOC, No Objection Certificate. A resident of the country where the person wants to go is required to sponsor him. This certificate is absolutely essential and is issued by a firm or an individual offering employment. Suppose these criminals receive two NOCs. They then show these to fifty different people charging them whatever they can afford. Most people don't mind paying up the amount demanded as they hope it will be ploughed back within a couple of months if they can get to the places where the employment is offered and the rest will be profit and a foot on the ever ascending escalator to comfort and luxury. The criminals then invest the fat sums they grab from these fifty people in their own business. There is a minimum limit of three months during which those who have paid cannot reclaim their money; so they're obliged to be patient. And this is considered normal as there are difficulties in sending people abroad. Passports are not immediately available, neither are visas. So three months of patience is not too much to ask for. Even then one's patience may be taxed, but it doesn't do to be over-impatient. Lobbies are employed to persuade politicians; the

Adam traders, as they are called, use the same methods. If someone becomes too impatient, there will be people around him to suggest that since he's waited for three months, can't he wait a little longer, now that his case is nearly through. That argument seems all very logical, so who's going to cast away their future out of impatience? Most wait, but if someone still insists, he's asked to accept a refund of five thousand taka, a small part of the money he's paid. He can't possibly ask them to refund the whole amount immediately. They'll tell him, very plausibly, that much of it has already been spent on his case. So one has to wait. There's no point in taking five thousand when you've paid forty. Many people have lost their everything in this fashion. Those who had sold their property in the village to raise the money are in deep trouble. I'd like to produce a witness before the court. Shaker Ali.'

As soon as he called the name, a man stood up, and everybody looked at him. 'You can take your seat now. I'll present you later,' the prosecutor told him.

'My lord, look at this unfortunate man,' he continued. 'You'll hear from his own lips later. I'll just say briefly that Shaker Ali comes from a fairly well-off peasant family. He's read Arts up to the intermediate level. He's the only educated member of the family; it's natural for him to have ambition; and it's not surprising that his old father wanted him to succeed. But the old man didn't think of the possible consequences. When the boy proposed the scheme, his father didn't have to accept it. But the old man was in a dilemma. You must remember that these criminals are sometimes successful in sending people abroad. Suppose one person in a village goes abroad. Thousands of taka are then dispatched to the village and news spreads that someone in the village earns thousands of taka. Not just that; when the fellow returns to the village after a year or two, he's a marvel to look at. He's dressed in an expensive suit, has an expensive wristwatch and a transistor set. His suitcase is filled with expensive clothes and such like. The family enjoys a virtual Eid festival. Who can keep his head cool at such spectacle? Land is a bigger bait. Land! Everybody's crazy about land in this country. Food, clothes and honour depend on this priceless object. After one such experience, news goes round that there's a remote place called Arabstan, the land of the Arabs, getting to which would mean the satisfaction of your life's ambitions, and it wouldn't take long either. You must be patient until you've reached the destination, but once you're in the court of the *Elahi* you should receive all you want. Everybody seeks salvation; how many are saved? But there your wishes are immediately fulfilled. The old man had seen such a young man in a neighbouring village. So why hesitate? He had other sons, sons who ploughed their own land and rented out a little for a share of the crop. Compared to others in the village, they were well-off. But things could have been even better. One college-educated brother could see not only to the present but to the future of their descendants. Meanwhile the confidence men were not inactive. If you can get a client from a village, you're going to get a cut from the thirty or forty thousand taka thus made. The agents pursue their interests wherever they find a chance. Shaker Ali's old father hasn't stopped crying. You've seen the boy. The defendant Qazi Alamin didn't take the money himself, someone from his gang did. He's now absconded, but the defendant has been seen with the absconder. Qazi Alamin has no licence to send people abroad, so he associated with those who did. He was particularly active as an exporter of women. He was in charge of some of these houses. Although the defendant hasn't admitted his guilt and has given other names — and it's possible that they're the real culprits — yet in the eyes of the law his offence cannot be condoned. Saburan is a simple country girl. She's given us some names and accompanied the police to some of the addresses. But these houses are now either abandoned or occupied by others. Yet the sentinels of the law are alert and the quarry will not escape. It's a question of time. They provided shelter for people before they were sent abroad. They had homes for the purpose. It appears from the defendant's confession that his work was confined to providing such shelter. There is no doubt that he's an abettor. For cheating, export and sale of men and women abroad, as well as abetting, the defendant will be charged under sections four hundred and twenty, three hundred and sixty-one, four hundred and ninety-eight, three hundred and forty-four, and seventy-one and seventy-two of the Penal Code. I have already described the perfidious activities he engaged in, and although he apparently lived like a gentleman, that concealed a filth inside which has now spilled out to spread across the world. Such despicable characters must be punished for the health of the nation, for the sake of law and order. This is my plea.'

The prosecutor had been impressive. His concern for morality and the public good had given his voice an edge of emotion which persisted even when it sank to a low pitch. Now a sombre atmosphere reigned in the court.

It was the defence lawyers' turn to cross-examine some witnesses. Ramiz Ali's name came up but the judicial clerk informed that he was ill and had applied for leave of absence with a medical certificate. It was tiffin hour by the time some unimportant witnesses had been cross-examined. The magistrate decided not to resume the case in the afternoon even though the next date of hearing was not until a fortnight later.

The case soon attracted wide attention through the newspaper reports of the clashes between the opposing lawyers. The visitors' gallery was regularly full to bursting; indeed, the crowd got so large that the magistrate had to force some people out. In the court-precinct, people were continually asking one another about the progress of the case. The lawyers' disputes became a source of witticism and sarcasm. Many unemployed young men thronged the court to witness the fun, and fellow victims of the trade on trial eagerly awaited verdicts of guilt. Soon the interest in the case became so great that newspaper reporters were desperate to get their reports into the following day's papers. Not a photo journalist missed out on taking photographs of Saburan and Qazi Alamin. Aware of this pitch of interest, the lawyers of the contending parties got so excited that one would blurt out a remark when his adversary was in the midstream of his statement. As things got complicated, Magistrate Karim found himself tangled in queries, protests and demands for interpretation of the finer points of the law. It was not hard to conclude that Qazi had been involved in the export of women to various countries, but it was also evident that such was the complexity of the business that it wouldn't have been possible without the help of many powerful and influential people. Indeed, Qazi Alamin once let it out that such complicated work was not possible on his own, that he was only an agent, providing shelter for a few men and women, that he was not supposed to know the whereabouts of those whom he encountered in other areas of the business. Saburan admitted that she used to go to various places but she only knew those places through Qazi. She didn't even know the numbers of those houses. Qazi used to give her some names, but it was hard for her to memorise the connection between the names and the faces, and that she didn't go out everyday. Someone used to go and pay a certain sum of money to Saburan's father. By the time the police got to know about it, the man had stopped going to the village. The police were hopeful that all the culprits would be rounded up, however exalted their social position. The pincers of the law were not inactive.

As examination and cross-examination crashed around the courtroom, the case came to be seen as a dramatic conflict between the public prosecutor, the defence lawyers Aftab Ali and Mahmud Hossain, and magistrate Sajedul Karim.

The public prosecutor was a massive and muscular man with an unusual swelling on his palms near the thumb. His bushy moustache and booming voice gave his speeches an exceptional resonance. Barrister Aftab Ali was, in this respect, his opposite. He was thin, although not sickly. What he lacked in the resonance of his voice he made up for in the pointedness of his argument. He was about sixty and had a fine moustache with a touch of grey. When he spoke he cast his eyes wide across the court. Mahmud Hossain looked much younger, no more than fifty years of age. He was stouter than Aftab, but much thinner than the public prosecutor. The cheeks of his round face glowed with health. When absorbed in legal argument, his hands automatically strayed towards his tie or some parts of his gown. When he needed help from his aide he slightly tilted his head and stretched out his arm. There was no trace of hurry about him, but his speech became faster when he sensed he was about to floor his adversary. The magistrate seemed an avatar of Vishnu. He was thin — and looked even thinner in his tightly fitting European clothes — and though he was in charge of the court, there was no trace of temper or haughtiness about him. His voice was soft, his manners mild. One expected words of love to emerge from that voice, never words of order. A quiet glance was the most that came from him, as if by his simple modesty he could subdue the over-assertiveness of the contending barristers. The three lawyers, in the heat of argument, abandoned the rituals of address, but the magistrate seemed not concerned about it. The truth was he found himself swimming so precariously in the cyclone of arguments that the thought of what judgment he would have to come up with, if this sort of thing continued, rather unnerved him. One had to be watchful of the loopholes of the law. Who likes to be criticised by a superior court?

As the case progressed, the two barristers for the defence seemed more and more like partners in a musical act in their response to the prosecutor's case, or involved in a relay race, each ready to run as soon as the other had handed on the baton.

'My lord,' the defence lawyer Mahmud Hossain began, 'the public prosecutor has shackled my client Qazi Alamin hand and foot with many sections of the Penal Code and is now waiting for the whiplashes of judgment. But it's well known, is it not, that you cannot prove a case on sheer guesswork. The ticket collectors at Dhaka railway station are able to tell you before anyone else that the population of the town is going up, but they cannot tell you in which areas it's going up: Azimpur, Dhanmondi, Santinagar, Rajarbag, Segunbagicha or Malibag. The truth of a proposition depends on empirical evidence. Circumstances indicate, but cannot prove anything with certainty. You need eyes for naked truth, eyes directed by a healthy brain. The eyes of the insane or the drunk see a lot, like for example a reservoir in that yard, but even if it was evident to him, it wouldn't be true, certainly not to the healthy and the sane. My client is allegedly a trader in women, an exporter of men and women to the Middle East; he is even tainted with the brush of a slaver. The lawyers on the other side have established their acumen for guesswork, like the ticket collectors of Dhaka railway station, but have not been able to focus on the actual reality of the situation. It is easy to tarnish a name, only a matter of words. If your lips, tongue and vocal cords are intact, you can tarnish a good name. But to establish the truth you need solid ground and a stock of hard evidence. The main thing is facts, but our opponents are concerned only with value judgments. So they put great emphasis on morality. But are morality and legality identical? They are certainly related, but the difference is by no means negligible. Cohabitation with one's wife is legal and there is nothing immoral about it, but in the public parks and sparse bushes it's illegal and punishable. Though moral values are there for the good of society, their object is the individual. The object of the law is communal and social life. Our opponents are unable to produce any evidence to prove that our clients have done anything illegal.

I want to bring this to the notice of the court. It has been repeated that my client is guilty of trading in men and women. There are citizens of this country held in the gaols of other countries and one also hears about the misfortunes of certain women through their letters, but there is no evidence that these unfortunate men and women are victims of my client's corrupt practices. And the charge of prostitution is entirely without foundation. This sort of charge cannot be established in a Muslim society without the testimony of four pious witnesses — and it must be remembered that the piety of the four men must be established first. It is not enough simply to witness the incident. The prosecuting lawyers drove a steamroller of charges without an eye to these aspects and they did so without let or hindrance. For their edification I'd like to...' Barrister Mahmud Hossain slightly tipped his neck towards his aide and said, 'It's marked in the Holy Quran, open at page...' He soon resumed, 'Allah, the Holy Lord, tells us in the Quran,' then turning to his colleague, he said, 'Mr Aftab Ali, you are an expert in Arabic and Persian, your pronunciation will be accurate, would you kindly read the Arabic text?'

'Mr Hossain,' the magistrate intervened, 'none of us understand Arabic. The Bengali translation should be enough.'

'So be it,' the barrister resumed. 'Chapter 24, Verse 4: "Those that defame honourable women and cannot produce four witnesses shall be given eighty lashes. No testimony of theirs shall be admissible, for they are great transgressors." You have now heard the injunction of the Holy Quran. Where are the witnesses? The public prosecutor himself said the police hadn't produced any eyewitnesses. It's all guessed from circumstances. But guesses are subject to doubt, and doubt implies inability to ascertain the truth of the matter.

'Another of my client's alleged crimes has been repeatedly proclaimed in this court: that he has reintroduced slavery in the twentieth century when the whole civilised world is free from this ignominy. It should be noted that those men and women who are said to have been sold to slavery have not brought any complaint against my client in the court. We have spoken to our client in prison in connection with the case. He is innocent — at least untarnished in this respect, he tells us. He has not been able to *prove* he is innocent. How else did so many unfortunate people get incarcerated in foreign gaols? Well, if you find a fruit lying under a tree, you'd assume that the fruit is from that tree. But if there are many trees close to one another, can you tell from which tree it has fallen? There is much talk of deceived men and women and their complaints. But is my client the only man left in this country? If he had sent the rest of his compatriots packing to live here on his own, it wouldn't be hard to find the culprit. But my question is: what's the population of this country? Besides, you need a licence to send people abroad. Well, aren't there others in possession of such licences? I don't need to say more. There's also a question about who passed the anti-slavery Bill and when. In the context of the present case one should give that a thought too. It's about a hundred and fifty years ago, a hundred and forty to be exact, the fifth bill to be passed by the East India Company was the Anti-slavery Act. It takes time to enforce a law after you have had it passed. It was enforced in Sylhet in 1879, in West Jalpaiguri and Duars in 1881 and in the hills of Garo, Khasia and Jayanti in 1889, that is, quite close to the twentieth century. One may feel curious about the northern regions of India. The law was enforced in Hajara, Peshawar, Kohat, Bannu, Dera Ismail Khan and Dera Ghazi Khan in 1886, that is, forty years had gone by before the law was enforced. The case of other countries is not entirely irrelevant. Slavery was abolished in Afghanistan in 1923, in Nepal in 1926, in Trans-Jordan and Iran in 1929, in Bahrain in 1937, in Saudi Arabia in 1952. It is unnecessary to extend the list. But are we in an independent country obliged to follow the laws of the Christian English? It should be remembered that my client is a Muslim.' Mahmud Hossain's speech was not over, but the impatient public prosecutor stood up and cried, without caring to address the court, 'A dealer in women cannot be a Muslim!'

The lawyers' eyes met, but Mahmud Hossain was calm, icy. He looked at Aftab Ali, who was sitting next to him. They must have had a dialogue with their eyes, for barrister Aftab Ali now stood up. Looking upward, he turned his neck both ways, as if to look down from above on what was happening below and to consider if making a reply would be casting pearls to the swine. Then he grabbed his gown at the neck and lifted it slightly, perhaps to ease the torment of sweat underneath. Then, promptly fixing the magistrate with a stare, he began, 'The state prosecutor has raised a valid question, a question of validity. Can a trader in women be a Muslim? His meaning is clear: an antisocial element gets expelled from his community.'

'Of course,' the impatient public prosecutor let out impatiently, still sitting.

'But, your honour, who's going to certify certainty in this matter?' Aftab Ali's voice was very quiet, without a hint of excitement. 'My lord, we must then say that thieves, cheats, pickpockets, lechers, self-seekers, the mendacious, the bad elements, traitors, punters, murderers, pimps, bribe-takers, cruel property-grabbers, etc. etc. are not Muslims.'

'Of course not,' the public prosecutor cried.

Taking no notice of him, barrister Ali continued, 'My lord, what did the Muslim League, that is, Mr. Jinnah, understand by the word Muslim? Of the millions who assembled under the flag of the Muslim League, were there no antisocial elements? Were they all honest and virtuous citizens? We know that by Muslim the Muslim League meant those born of Muslim parents, be they thieves, lechers or murderers. Their moral quality was irrelevant. The lists of voters were prepared that way, so thousands of antisocial elements got into the party. Cheats, pickpockets, lechers, self-seekers, the mendacious and the bad elements, traitors, punters, murderers, pimps, bribe-takers, property-grabbers, the hedonists, the informers — and so on and so on — found shelter in the Muslim League because it was not found necessary to ask who a Muslim was. But my client has been thrown out of the community of Muslims before being proved guilty.'

'Your honour,' the public prosecutor had risen to his feet during the brief pause in barrister Aftab Ali's speech, 'the defence lawyer doesn't know the definition of the word Muslim. It's unnecessary to pursue what is irrelevant.'

As Maqbool Ahmed sat down, Aftab Ali uttered the word 'definition' three times, though it was not clear whether from surprise or from contempt. Now he raised his voice, 'My lord, the Muslim League, that is, Mr. Jinnah, did well to use a working definition. This is not the place to decide whether the consequences were good or bad, but let the logicians in the other party know that definitions don't come easy. It's not easy to define the word Muslim. The court must allow me to return to the past a little. Only thirty years ago there was a fierce riot in the Punjab in Pakistan. In the subcontinent when we talk of riots, we usually mean riots between Hindus and Muslims. But this was a riot between Muslims and Muslims. Muslims are a religious group, but there are subgroups within the group. Trouble starts in the family when you take a concubine on top of a wife. So there was nothing unusual in a riot between Sunni Muslims and Ahmedi Muslims, though the fierceness of the riot would horrify any sane man. It's hard to imagine that a little difference of opinion within the same religious community could lead to such murder, looting, robbery and arson. But believe me, over five thousand people died in the province within a few days. The Ahmedis were a minority, so they bore the brunt of it. Sometimes many people were hurled into a room, which was then set on fire, and all in the name of religion. But the Punjab riots took place thirty years ago. The reason I have taken so long to introduce the subject is that these riots offered an opportunity to arrive at a definition of the word Muslim. Troops had to be called out to stop the Punjab riots. Then the Government appointed an inquiry commission, of which Justice Munir was the Chairman and Justice Rustam Kayani a member. The official title of the report is *Report of Inquiry into the Punjab Riots of 1953*, but it's popularly known as the Munir Report.'

Barrister Ali paused briefly and stretched out his arm towards his colleague, who handed him a book. Holding the book in his hand, Aftab Ali resumed: 'On this occasion a number of *ulema* and chiefs of religious organisations were invited. At one point of the inquiry, Justice Munir asked them to define the word Muslim. Everyone was an authority in religious matters. There is no need to rehearse each definition. It will suffice if I quote the dialogue between Justice Munir and Moulana Badayuni. This is how it goes:

Maulana Abdul Hamid Badayuni, President, Jami'-ul-Ulama-i-Pakistan:

"Q.— Who is a Musalman according to you?

A.— A person who believes in the *zarooriyat-i-din* is

called a *momin* and every *momin* is entitled to be called a Musalman.

Q.— What are these *zarooriyat-i-din*?

A.— A person who believes in the five pillars of Islam and who believes in the *rasalat* of our Holy Prophet fulfils the *zarooriyat-i-din*.

Q.— Have any other actions, apart from the five *arakan*, anything to do with a man being a Muslim or being outside the pale of Islam?

(*Note* — Witness has been explaining that by actions are meant those rules of moral conduct which in modern society are accepted as correct.)

A.— Certainly.

Q.— Then you will not call a person a Muslim who believes in *arakan-i-khamsa* and the *rasalat* of the prophet but who steals other people's things, embezzles property entrusted to him, has an evil eye on his neighbour's wife and is guilty of the grossest ingratitude to his benefactor?

A.— Such a person, if he has the belief indicated, will be a Muslim despite all this".

'There are other definitions given by other religious authorities, but they are all different. So Justice Munir comments, and I will quote from page 218 of the report: "Keeping in view the several definitions given by the *ulema*, need we make any comment except that no two learned divines are agreed on this fundamental. If we attempt our own definition as each learned divine has done and that definition differs from that given by all others, we unanimously go out of the fold of Islam. And if we adopt the definition given by any one of the *ulema*, we remain Muslim according to the view of that *alim* but *kafirs* according to the definition of everyone else."

'My lord, we may now leave the Munir Report behind.' Aftab Ali handed the book to his aide and continued the train of his argument: 'The point I'd like to make is that in the matter of definition of the word Muslim one should not go beyond what Jinnah and others since have done. That is, we'll call one a Muslim if one is born in a Muslim family. What is my client's crime? He has been called a slaver. Slavery is considered an unlawful business. But who made these laws? The Christian English who, in common Islamic parlance, are called *nasara*, that is, the inhabitants of Nazareth. Muslims are not bound by the laws of the *nasara*. We are guided by the words and practices of our dear prophet Hazrat Muhammad Mustafa Sallellahe-s-salam. Over and above there is the word of God in the Holy Quran. We'll not be answerable to other laws, particularly in a free country. What the Christian rulers did is beyond the pale of our judgment now. Slavery is not condemned in the Quran or the Sunnah as a hateful crime, although there are repeated instructions not to be cruel to slaves. Indeed, we can appreciate the impact of Islam if we compare the situation of the slave before and after the advent of Islam. The slaves in the gold and copper mines in ancient Rome worked under unbearable conditions for bare subsistence until they dropped dead. In Muslim countries they were employed in domestic work. But there are no instructions in Islam to abolish slavery. Even if my client had slave girls, assuming that he did, wherein lies his crime?'

Magistrate Sajedul Karim now intervened: 'Mr Ali, don't forget the times.'

'My lord, the holy books are not so fragile as to be tied to time. The truth contained in them is eternal, against which time pits its head in vain. Yet my client is accused. Read the twentieth chapter of the thirteenth part of the holy Meshkath; there you won't find slavery condemned as unlawful. At the end of the eighteenth century, Muslim rulers of Africa joined hands with the Christians in the slave trade. My client's offence cannot be called deplorable, although the public prosecutor has cast offensive adjectives even before the judgment. It has also been said that this kind of trade would not have been possible if the girls were not made to sell their bodies first. But what is the crime in treating a slave girl as a slave girl?'

Aftab Ali turned to the public gallery as well as to the magistrate. The index finger of his left hand was raised as if he was expecting an answer from somebody. Then his eyes fell on his companion and a silent dialogue was conducted between the two. Barrister Ali sat down as if he had nothing more to say, but Mahmud Hossain stood up immediately. His fat fleshy neck swelled up a little as an ironic smile formed on one side of his mouth. His soft resonant voice immediately filled the room.

'I want to make it even clearer, for those who have any doubts, that whatever the social position of slave girls in Islam, there is no restriction to their use as women. I want to quote from the word of God, the Holy Quran. Our Holy Lord Allah says in the fifth verse of the thirty-third chapter, in surah Ahzab — I'll not quote the whole verse as just a small part of the Holy Word is enough for our present argument — "Prophet," I quote, "We have made lawful to you the wives whom you have granted dowries and the slave girls whom Allah has given you as booty." It's clear that my client's offence is not so great after all. One could, of course, raise the question as to whether these girls were actually bought from their guardians but could not condemn slavery as a punishable, hateful crime. Far be it that there is any law superior to the word of God; even to imagine such a possibility is a great sin. My lord, these slaves were not wives. In Arabia they were called mothers of children. They were mothers of one's children but not wives. That is, they did not receive the honour of a wife. There are no valid charges against my client. One heard in this very courtroom a demand for his punishment under six or seven sections of the Penal Code. It doesn't seem that the prosecutor has looked at the fundamentals. What's the foundation of these charges? Can one build without foundation? Of course one can, but only in imagination. If we assume that we have gathered here to compose a tale or a poem, then, my lord, it's meaningless to proceed any further. If we arrive at judgment before the hearing there is very little the lawyers can do. Another charge has been brought against my client that he has — yes, I'll say 'he', as there is only one defendant, although the state witness has mentioned others, some of whom have stayed in the wings and some absconded — that this single person has sent people abroad with forged passports and visas. But why does one need these documents? When one travels from one country to another one needs permission to do so. Now there are many different communities in the world, not all Muslim. If you are travelling to a country inhabited by a different community, then you obviously need passports and visas in compliance with the laws of that country. But why should one need visas to go to a Muslim country? Muslims are one nation. Muslims do not believe in the geographical nationalism of the West. There isn't a hint of nationalism in the Quran or the Hadith. Remember the last *khutba* of our dear prophet where he said that Muslims should not be Arabs or non-Arabs. Is there any room for geographical nationalism after that? Following the ways of the Christians and other nonbelievers, we have deviated from the true path. Muslims are a nation, the Western concept of nationhood doesn't apply to Muslims. You can't have forgotten the poet Iqbal, who declared, China and Arabia are ours and so is India; we are Muslims and the whole world is our home. Although this has not been realised, because there are Christians, Jews and nonbelievers, how can we apply Western standards to Muslim countries? It's true that Muslims of other countries need visas to perform the Haj, but why should people need visas to go to Mecca and Medina? Are the rulers of these countries obeying our dear prophet's final *khutba*. What amazing practice of the sunnah?'

Mahmud Hossain did not usually get sentimental when speaking in court. He stayed on the firm ground of the law, and even when he occasionally got emotional, it was not reflected in his manner, but on this occasion he strayed far from his usual composure. 'My lord, nationalism, nation-state: these are European ideas and concepts. We'd be non-believers if we accepted them. If anybody has done so in the past he should seek forgiveness from all-forgiving Allah. Muslims are one nation. How else did Pakistan come into being? I'd therefore conclude that my client is not guilty. For no visas should be required for those travelling from one Muslim country to another. Lying in the matters opposed to the tenets of Islam cannot be very sinful. Allah will condone such sins. So I'd say my client is not guilty.

'My lord, I'd like to attract your attention to one or two more things. Why are the eyes of all poor Muslims drawn to the Middle East? One should remember that ugly women don't get raped, but everybody is attracted to a pretty woman. Muslims other than those of the Middle East are poor. Their eyes are drawn to the Middle East because of its recently acquired wealth. Oil has been in store under the ground from Baba Adam's time. You need brain oil to get that oil in the ground up to the surface. But the brain oil of the Middle East has been dried up because of an absence of drive, for hundreds of years. The rulers of those countries have let Islam be distorted, tarnished, condemned for hundreds of years. But the Christians have not been sitting around. Their brains throbbed with energy, they started getting the oil out. The Middle East is now bursting with wealth thanks to the Christians. The Middle East's never seen so much wealth. But their cultural life has been dead for centuries. So they don't know how to use their newly acquired wealth. The tendencies of the new rich have seized them. They cannot think of anything beyond their stomachs and genitals. It's been said that girls are being sent there for economic activities — and it has to be admitted that the imagination of the new rich is confined between a woman's thighs, which is perhaps natural, as they know no better. Like a sewerage system, there has to to be some drains for the satisfaction of carnal desire, otherwise the whole town could be contaminated. Had they had their own red light areas, there would have been no need to import women from abroad. But the idea of social reform is unnatural in a society closed for centuries. So the new rich of the Middle East go to the free societies of the West for a moral holiday. My poor client is a victim of history. I've already said that an ugly woman does not get raped. The great wealth created by the brain oil of the Christians has now become an important element in spreading sinfulness in the world. One's way of life changes with the acquisition of wealth. If you have good food and no healthy social environment, lechery will find its way in. Potatoes were imported to Europe in the sixteenth century, so Europeans had their food problem solved. They grew fatter. Importation of potatoes, according to a historian, caused even their penises to inflate. A similar historic change is being repeated in the Middle East because of the influx of inestimable wealth. With a strong cultural life, a man keeps his future in mind. The Middle East today is so engrossed with the present that it does not care about the future. So they indulge in *la dolce vita*. The proof is that the state of Israel was created in 1948 with a quarter of a million Jews, who threw out the native inhabitants of Palestine. They had the support of Anglo-American imperialism. For over thirty years they've been grabbing one area after another and one hundred twenty million Muslims have been watching the fun. One hundred and twenty million! Yes, one hundred and twenty million. Which means three per cent of the people of the Middle East are giving the rest a bloody backside. Just look at the conduct of the ninety seven per cent. The rulers of these states claim to be protectors of Islam, but they show no urge to protect their Palestinian brothers. Why? Because they are tied to the chains of their wealth. Their great wealth is invested in American and British banks. So they verbally sympathise with their Palestinian friends but do not get to the battlefield for fear of annoying their Christian friends. They cannot imagine that they themselves may fall victim to the Christians in the future, because they are incapable of imagining. Their brain oil has dried up over the centuries. So they're drawn to *la dolce vita* and their women have to be imported from abroad. It shouldn't take one long to understand the power of the social cyclone of which my client is a victim. My client is not guilty. He's been charged under section 340 for illegal detention and under 372/73 and others for illegal trading in women. But these laws cannot apply to Muslims unless a foundation for them has been established. I urge the court to take all the details into consideration. I'd also pray for a prompt conclusion of the case, as months have already passed in cross examination and other investigations.'

Barrister Mahmud Hossain took his seat, next to Aftab Ali. As they shook hands under the table, he whispered, 'All praise to Allah.'

Such, roughly, was the debate which took place in the court. To the public, the defence lawyers seemed like a pair of wrestlers on the attack. Once in a while the public prosecutor tried to corner them, but they were so quick that even when their adversary had thrown them down and put the weight of his body on them, they could reverse the position in a moment and get back on top. The whole town was excited and eagerly awaited the verdict. Needless to say, the press had been ever present. Trainee lawyers, whose activities were still limited to attending the courts, had not missed a day's hearing; senior lawyers attended in their free time. Later, educated people in general were stirred by the case and many came along.

All that remained was the judgment, but the magistrate, giving himself plenty of time to decide, fixed the next date for the court session a month later. This was unusual. It was customary to deliver judgments promptly, often the day after, or at most a week later if there were complications. But on this occasion a month was taken; there were clearly some knotty problems. The curious were impatient but they had to wait.

In the event, the judgment was never given.

In an insignificant place in the court columns, its heading only one column wide and in a type not prominent enough to attract attention, there was the story:

Death of the prisoner under trial. The piece was brief. A prisoner involved in a case about dealing in people had been found dead in prison. It said nothing about the cause or circumstances of his death. Generally, sudden deaths of prisoners greatly stirred journalists. Such news usually made stories for days, increasing the sales of the newspaper. Sometimes traces of an incident like this could be seen floating around in the newspapers for weeks. But this particular news seemed to have paled into insignificance on the day of its publication. There were still a few rumours, it is true. A prisoner under trial had died in prison. At least the jail authorities could have been asked to explain, some people said, but nothing of the sort happened. Others said there must be big guns behind the prisoner who had conspired to bring about the incident. Some thought that if you sinned, your soul wouldn't rest, self-reproach being a kind of inner burning that kept alive like an apparently dormant volcano; in such situations one might commit suicide and if one wanted to die it wouldn't be difficult to find a way. Rumours of one kind or another. Naturally there were differences in view between members of the legal profession and members of the general public.

Doubts deepened when nobody came to collect the prisoner's body after the authorities asked the prisoner's relatives and even his lawyers to do so. So the prison authorities were forced to take the responsibility for his funeral. This much was true, the rest rumour.

As the main defendant was dead, there was no necessity to deliver the judgment. However, the case rumbled on for a time as, according to the state witness, some offenders had absconded. In the end, no one was quite sure whether it had ended or not.

CHAPTER FOUR

'Whose face did I see this morning?' Saburan asked herself repeatedly, without an answer.

She had not expected to be freed from the prison before the trial was over. But the unthinkable happened when an assistant jailer, accompanied by a constable, came to tell her that she was free to go home. The police had informed the court authorities that as the absconders had not yet been arrested, and it was uncertain when they would be, there was no point in having the state witness rotting in prison. She could go home if she wanted to. When the arrests were made, she would be asked to appear in court.

Saburan nearly broke down. The world was a maze and she had made friends in prison. They gathered round her when they heard that she had been freed. What would she tell them? The jailer and the constable were waiting at the door. Saburan said farewell to them, one by one. Living together, she had developed an affection for each one.

Then she quickly got ready — she had only a couple of saris with her. She repeatedly wiped her tears. She remembered Khala, who had given her courage, without which she might have died worrying.

There was little delay at the jail gate. They had her two gold bangles and ten taka which were refunded to her as soon as she made her thumb mark on a sheet of paper. She walked out of the gate, facing the wind. There were no walls round her. Yet walls rushed towards her.

Where would she go now? Her old address no longer existed. She remembered her first mistress. Would she get a day's rest if she went to her? She was an honest and sympathetic woman. But so many years had passed. Perhaps she mightn't be there any more or she had died or something had happened to her. So much depended on chance; she would have to give it a try.

Fortune smiled on Saburan. Her old mistress not only let her stay, she helped her in ways that Saburan would always want to remember. She knew the area and she had ten taka, so she had no difficulty in paying the rickshaw fare. Saburan, of course, said nothing of her past. She arranged with her former mistress that she would work for her when she got back from her village. If there wasn't a vacancy then, perhaps she could find her one somewhere else. Her old mistress not only allowed her to stay for two days, she even took her to the jewellers to sell her bangles for her. 'If you go and sell them on your own,' she said, 'they'll suspect you. They won't understand that you've made them from years of toil. Perhaps they'll call the police, thinking that you've stolen them from some house.' Saburan wondered why all the people in the world couldn't be like her mistress. She had seen so many bitches in her life as a maid servant. She was moved and thankful.

The price of gold had gone up, so she got two and a half thousand taka. Saburan fancied a tin box with a rose painted on it, but her mistress dissuaded her. 'You're carrying money, don't attract trouble. There are thieves and swindlers on the road. Put it in your bundle, a large *gamtcha* or sari should do.'

Saburan did not buy much. Two lungis for her father, a

couple of saris each for herself and her stepmother, two tablets of soap, a bottle of hair oil and some titbits. She would return to her village like a country girl. She bought a pair of sandals, but they were for her father, not for herself.

Saburan knew the railway station and how to get to her village. Qazi had told her this. He hadn't lied to her; her father had received money every month. During the trial she heard that the man who paid the money had not been to see her father for the last three months. Saburan realised that he had feared arrest; that was obvious enough to her.

She held her bundle carefully. She had no trouble buying her ticket. It wasn't busy. She had passed through the gate when she heard someone call her from behind: 'Listen, dear.'

She looked back: an old woman, but quite stout and hardy. One could see from her teeth that she chewed much *pan*. Her eyes were rather small and without sympathy.

'Are you calling me?'

'Yes, dear. Where are you going?'

'Hijalia.'

'That's next to my village.'

'We'll go together.'

Saburan was at first much relieved that she had a companion. They sat together. The old woman was keen to talk, but Saburan would not go beyond yes, no. She looked at the fields and trees from the train window and sensed inside her a restless heart. How was Bap? He hadn't received any money for six or seven months now. How was his health? Had he gone grey? Her stepmother was a good woman, but God knows what had become of her. Such thoughts crowded upon her and she found no consolation in the old woman's words.

Saburan had dozed off from the rocking of the train. She

was startled by the old woman's call: 'Get up, dear. We're there.'

Saburan did not care to ask which station it was. Why ask if they were going to the same place? But as soon as the train set off again the old woman cried, 'Don't panic, dear, but we've got off two stations too soon.'

'What are we going to do now?' Saburan's head swam.

'Don't panic. The next train is at night. It's not a good idea to travel at night. We'll go tomorrow morning. My sister lives round here, we can stay with her for the night.'

Saburan felt helpless and annoyed with the old woman. But at least her sister's village was not far and they could get there in a rickshaw. It was not possible to spend the night in an unknown railway station, particularly when she was carrying all her worldly possessions other than her youth. Her whole future was in her bundle, as well as her father's.

As they were about to set off in a rickshaw, two young men, who had got off the same train, walked up to them, addressed the old woman as auntie, exchanged a word or two with her and then walked away.

Nobody has seen Saburan since. Who would be curious about the whereabouts of an obscure country girl? The people of her village heard that she had disappeared during police enquiries. Later a few suspects in the old case were arrested. Saburan was required to identify them, so the police went to her village. When they could not find her there, they conducted a search and made enquiries, in the course of which one or two passersby reported having seen a young woman with a bundle and an old woman together at the railway station but beyond that they couldn't say more.

Saburan never returned to her father.

AFTERWORD

Osman Jamal

Shaukat Osman

Shaukat Osman is the most eminent writer in Bangladesh. Since the mid-forties, when he appropriated for Bengali literature the hitherto largely ignored life of the Muslim peasant and urban poor, Osman has had a tireless literary career, producing over seventy volumes of fiction, drama, poetry, essays and juvenilia. His work has been translated in several languages of the Indian subcontinent, including English. A number of his short stories have been translated into European languages, including Russian, German and Norwegian. *The State Witness* is one of the two novels being published in Britain this year, the other being *Janani*.

Shaukat Osman was born in 1917 in a village called Sabalsinghapur in the district of Hoogley, now in West Bengal. Son of a pious Muslim farmer and artisan, he went to a *maktab*, an Islamic primary school, until he was twelve, but matriculated in 1933 from the liberal Anglo-Persian Division of Calcutta Alia Madrassa. He graduated in Economics from Calcutta St. Xavier's College and went on to read Bengali Literature at Calcutta University for his Masters. In 1942 he was appointed Lecturer at Calcutta Institute of Commerce. Migrating to the eastern wing of Pakistan (Bangladesh since 1971) following the partition of India in 1947, he continued teaching until he retired in 1972.

Shaukat Osman's first major novel, and probably his best to date, is *Janani* (Mother) (1945-46), an English translation of which is being published by Heinemann in November 1993. In this novel the core story of a mother crushed between the conflicting claims of her love for her children and her honour is embedded in a realistic evocation of a Bengal village, seen from the implicit perspective of a child. Another significant work of this period is *Bani Adam (Adam's Children)* (1946). Incomplete when it was first published in the Eid issue of *Azad*, this 'torso', as the author describes it, remains in its portrayal of the life of the urban poor an unsurpassed example of rugged realism. The short stories Osman wrote during the forties, collected in two volumes, *Pinjrapole* and *Junu Apa and other stories*, both published in 1951, consolidated his reputation as a major writer of this region.

Osman's next important novel was published in 1962, a few years after General Ayub Khan had taken power in Pakistan in a military coup. *The Laughter of the Slave,* (in Kabir Choudhury's translation) seeks in Haroun-al-Rashid's Bagdad an allegorical frame to condemn the cultural policy of the military ruler, who tried to bribe the intelligentsia into submission. Another novel in this mode, *The King and the Serpents,* (in Roshaida Khatun's translation) tells the story of how King Zahuk of Persia, cursed to carry round his neck a pair of serpents, who must be fed on human brains, is freed by a man of the people. Allegory, as well as symbolism, is also employed in some of the short stories he wrote during this period, collected in three volumes, *The Stone Tablet* (1964), *Perspectives* (1968) and *Dilemma* (1968).

Osman returns to realism during, and following, the Muktijuddo, the Bangladesh War of Liberation. *A Farewell to Hell* (1971), *The Wolf Forest* (1973) and *Jolangi* (1974) were written either in exile in Calcutta during the war or immediately following it. Too close in time to the experience for an adequate perspective, these novellas of atrocities and heroism remain acts of protest. Some of the short stories written during this period and collected in two volumes,

Two Soldiers (1973) and *If You Were Born in Bengal* (1975), are certainly more sucessful.

The murder of Sheikh Mujibur Rahman, the founding father of Bangladesh, in 1974, and the eventual military takeover, shattered Osman's dream of political, social and cultural liberation. The diaries he kept during the years of exile following these political developments are now being published in a 830-page volume called *Mujibnagar: the Sequel*, Mujibnagar being the name of the largely mythical capital of Bangladesh during the war of 1971. Osman goes back to the allegorical mode in *The Insect Cage* (1983), the story of a village under an oppressive cloud of insects, interminably shutting out the sun. This theme of alienation, of man in the face of powers he can neither comprehend nor control, is carried over into the real world of *The State Witness* (1986), which is also a satire on religious hypocrisy.

The allegorical mode blends into historical phantasy in a novella called *Assassins* (1991), where a sort of debate between religious orthodoxy and secularism is rehearsed when Dara Shuko and Aurangzeb, both sons of Emperor Shah Jehan, are summoned from the dead so that Dara can lead his orthodox Muslim younger brother (who ruled India for fifty years) along the corridors of Indian history, pointing accusingly at the harmful consequences of religious orthodoxy. In the title stories of *The Master and his Dog* (1990) and *God's Adversary* (1993) Osman again takes recourse to symbolism and allegory to attack social and political targets.

A committed writer and intellectual of the Enlightenment tradition, who calls himself a humanist, Osman devotes much of his time and energy to extra-literary struggle against obscurantism, religious bigotry and political oppression. He considers this unavoidable for a writer or intellectual of the third world. 'In my long trek from *The Laughter of the Slave* to *God's Adversary*, he recently wrote to a young writer, 'I have nowhere allowed my flag of protest to be brought down.'

Photograph by Khurshid Alam